Cast of Characters

Diana Prescott. An aspiring actress, she's run away from her domineering father to find success on the New York stage. Instead, she finds two bodies in a boarding house as well as an irritating suitor.

Quincy Prescott. Di's irate papa, who successfully runs a pea canning factory and less successfully his daughter's life.

Dennis Livingstone. Di thinks he's her father's stooge, sent to woo her home. Appearances can be deceiving.

Other Boarding House Residents

Mrs. Lulu Markham. The Boarding House owner. She has many rules and enforces all of them with a firm hand.

Barbara Markham. Her daughter and Diana's best friend. She has dark eyes and natural dark curls.

Grace Firebuck and **Mary Eustace**. Two school teachers on the wrong side of thirty.

Misses Imogene and **Opal Rostrum.** Thin, gray, and elderly boarders.

Alvin Mott. Mrs. Markham's brother-in-law, he's an elderly pensioner.

Camille. A sixtyish former actress.

Miss Giddens. An old lady with poor table manners.

Neville Ward. A bachelor.

Evie and **Kate.** Maids.

The Police

Inspector Dodd. He's in charge.

Sergeant Schmaltz. He growls a lot.

Books by Constance & Gwenyth Little

The Grey Mist Murders (1938)*
Black-Headed Pins (1938)*
The Black Gloves (1939)*
Black Corridors (1940)*
The Black Paw (1941)*
The Black Shrouds (1941)*
The Black Thumb (1942)*
The Black Rustle (1943)
The Black Honeymoon (1944)*
Great Black Kanba (1944)*
The Black Eye (1945)*
The Black Stocking (1946)*
The Black Goatee (1947)
The Black Coat (1948)*
The Black Piano (1948)
The Black Smith (1950)
The Black House (1950)
The Blackout (1951)
The Black Dream (1952)
The Black Curl (1953)
The Black Iris (1953)

*reprinted by the Rue Morgue Press
as of November 2002

The
Black
Shrouds

by
Constance & Gwenyth Little

The Rue Morgue Press
Boulder, Colorado

Printed at Johnson Printing
Boulder, Colorado

The Rue Morgue Press
P.O. Box 4119
Boulder, CO 80306

PRINTED IN THE UNITED STATES OF AMERICA

About the Littles

Although all but one of their books had "black" in the title, the 21 mysteries of Constance (1899-1980) and Gwenyth (1903-1985) Little were far from somber affairs. The two Australian-born sisters from East Orange, New Jersey, were far more interested in coaxing chuckles than in inducing chills from their readers.

Indeed, after their first book, *The Grey Mist Murders*, appeared in 1938, Constance rebuked an interviewer for suggesting that their murders weren't realistic by saying, "Our murderers strangle. We have no sliced-up corpses in our books." However, as the books mounted, the Littles did go in for all sorts of gruesome murder methods—"horrible," was the way their own mother described them—which included the occasional sliced-up corpse.

But the murders were always off stage and tempered by comic scenes in which bodies and other objects, including swimming pools, were constantly disappearing and reappearing. The action took place in large old mansions, boarding houses, hospitals, hotels, or on trains or ocean liners, anywhere the Littles could gather together a large cast of eccentric characters, many of whom seemed to have escaped from a Kaufman play or a Capra movie. The typical Little heroine—each book was a stand-alone—often fell under suspicion herself and turned detective to keep the police from slapping the cuffs on. Whether she was a working woman or a spoiled little rich brat, she always spoke her mind, kept her rather sarcastic sense of humor, and got her man, both murderer and husband. But if marriage was in the offing, it was always on her terms and the vows were taken with more than a touch of cynicism. Love was grand, but it was even grander if the husband could either pitch in with the cooking and cleaning or was wealthy enough to hire household help.

The Littles wrote all their books in bed—"Chairs give one backaches," Gwenyth complained—with Constance providing detailed plot outlines while Gwenyth did the final drafts. Over the years that pattern changed somewhat, but Constance always insisted that Gwen "not mess up my clues." Those clues were everywhere, and the Littles made sure there were no loose ends. Seemingly irrelevant events were revealed to be of major significance in the final summation. The plots were often preposterous, a fact often recognized by both the Littles and their characters, all of whom seem to be winking at the reader, almost as if sharing a private joke. You just have to accept the fact that there are different natural laws in that wacky universe created by these sisters.

The Littles published their two final novels, *The Black Curl* and *The Black Iris*, in 1953, and if they missed writing after that, they were at least able to devote more time to their real passion—traveling. The two made at least three trips around the world at a time when that would have been a major undertaking. For more information on the Littles and their books, see the introductions by Tom & Enid Schantz to The Rue Morgue Press editions of *The Black Gloves* and *The Black Honeymoon.*

CHAPTER ONE

OUTSIDE IT HAD BEGUN TO SNOW, and the early November dusk was already closing in. Barbara had turned on several lights in the huge, old-fashioned drawing room and was helping me to rehearse my part while we had the place to ourselves. She had even touched a match to the coal fire that was ready-made in the grate under the marble mantel, while I looked on with awe and breathless pleasure. Her mother's rule forbade that fire being lighted so much as a minute before half-past five in the afternoon, and since Mrs. Lulu Markham ran a superior hostelry with a firm hand there were a good many rules which were pretty strictly enforced.

The coals were glowing comfortably, and I stretched my chilled hands to them while I shook my head at Barbara. "You'll catch hell if she finds out."

"Oh, come on," she said impatiently. "You might as well go through this again. Someone is certain to come in in a minute, and we'll have to stop. And I don't care what Mama says—you can't expect people to play South Sea Island parts when they're freezing to death."

I decided that if Barbara ever got to be a famous actress someone should write into her biography that she had been willing to dare death and destruction for her art. Because Mrs. Markham could be politely terrifying if you broke her rules—and her daughter was in no way more privileged than the boarders.

As far as that goes, I had braved a good deal for art, myself. My father owns a canning factory upstate New York—he cans peas—and his idea was that I should settle down, get married, and reproduce myself. And all I ever wanted was to be a famous actress. We had argued it back and forth for several years, but Papa is extraordinarily pigheaded, and at last I had to defy him. When my mother died, many years ago, she left me a small income. It amounts to a little over a hundred a month, so I told Papa I was going to New York, enter a dramatic school, and live on my own income. And he was mean enough to let me—live on the income, I mean.

Mrs. Markham's place, an old-fashioned brownstone front in the West Eighties, had been recommended to me, so I engaged a room, enrolled in a dramatic school, and waited for Papa to loosen up. But he proved unusually obstinate, even for him. I sent him one of Mrs. Markham's dinner menus—but all I received by way of reply was a letter telling me that it would be good for my figure and didn't I remember Aunt Lillian who weighed three hundred pounds and had once been a slim young thing like me. He went on to say that I wouldn't get one cent as long as I persisted in playing the fool but that if I came home and behaved myself I might have an ermine coat and a few other things. He added that I did not resemble Maxine Elliott in the least and would certainly be laughed off the boards if, through somebody's mistake, I got as far as treading them. I slapped back a sarcastic page or two asking if he expected me to wear the ermine coat to the Elks' ball and how was I to keep the moths out of it for the rest of the year. There was no answer to that one for at least three weeks because Papa is an Elk and proud of it.

Barbara and I had paired off from almost the beginning of my stay at Mrs. Markham's. For one thing, we fancied ourselves ensemble, since she had dark eyes and dark brown natural curls, while my hair is fair and straight and my eyes blue. And then we discovered that we had the same ambition, although in Barbara's case there was no fight about it. Mrs. Markham was a widow, and her boardinghouse supported her comfortably, but she held an inheritance in trust for her daughter, and Barbara was to receive the income—nearly a hundred a month—when she reached the age of twenty-one. She was twenty—several years younger than I— and had only a year to wait. Mrs. Markham had said that she might go to dramatic school as soon as she received the money but that she must support herself on it too. In the meantime Barbara helped me with my homework and tried to learn what she could in advance.

Our bedrooms were so small that Barbara and I preferred the vast, ugly spaces of the drawing room whenever we could have it to ourselves. But we were usually interrupted, and that November afternoon was no exception. The two schoolteachers, Grace Firebuck and Mary Eustace, came stamping in with a powdering of snow gleaming on their fur collars.

Grace looked at us, laughed, and began to quote Shakespeare with gestures. Mary saw the fire and exclaimed, "Good God! My watch is half an hour slow!"

Barbara flung herself onto a couch and pulled out a cigarette. "Pay no attention, Diana. They're simply jealous. And not at all funny."

"My dear young girl," said Grace cheerfully, "play acting for people who are too bored or too meager of mind to find their own amusement is a far less important work than guiding the unfolding minds and souls of little children."

Mary removed her galoshes, pushed a chair practically into the fire, and sat down with a comfortable sigh. "If I never saw another little mind unfolding," she said with a noisy yawn, "it would still be too soon. I wish I had a little husband to guide."

"Can't you ever get the men off your mind?" Grace asked amiably.

"Not any more than you can. Only I admit it, and you won't."

"I can't see why you girls want to get married," I said, frowning thoughtfully. "You're both doing so well and—"

"How old are you?" Mary asked abruptly.

"I'm twenty-four but I don't see—"

"You don't see very far," Mary finished without malice. "Grace and I are over the thirty line—only just, of course—and we're getting panicky."

"Pest!"

We looked around to where Grace was peering through the stiff lace curtains, apparently at the brownstone steps outside. She whispered excitedly, without turning her head, "The answer to all my shy girlish dreams. He's standing out there on the stoop, holding a suitcase—and getting snowed on, poor lamb."

Barbara and I started up, but Mary beat us to the window, and though we pushed and shoved we couldn't see much over their shoulders.

"Selling magazines, probably," Barbara said, turning away.

Grace and Mary abandoned the window and quietly made for the heavy black portieres that filled the arch leading from the hall to the drawing room. Barbara and I followed and could hear a masculine voice arranging with Mrs. Markham for a room with board. He finished by asking at what time dinner would be served and then apparently followed Evie, a combination housemaid and waitress, up the stairs.

Grace and Mary fell back from the portieres and stared at each other.

"He's eating here, under this very roof, and in the same room with us—tonight!" Grace murmured in an awed voice.

Mary drew a deep breath and then glanced at Barbara and me. "What's to be done with the interference here?" she asked abruptly.

Grace shook her head. "I wish we had enough money to ship them off on a cruise—but poverty necessitates makeshifts, so I suppose the best we can do is to send them out to dinner and the movies."

"I don't want to go to the movies tonight," I said hastily.

"No," said Barbara, shaking back her curls, "I want to have dinner here and see the pretty man."

Grace merely said, "Tut-tut," and fished out some money.

Actually, they did pack us off, and with the greatest of ease. Teachers seem to develop a way of telling people to do things—and getting results. Barbara may have given a thought to her mother and the drawing-room fire—but I was simply stampeded.

Just before we left the Misses Imogene and Opal Rostrum caught up with us and timidly asked Barbara if she would change their library book. This was a fairly frequent chore for Barbara, and since she had to be courteous to the guests she could not very well get out of it.

"I don't believe Uncle Alvin has read it yet," she said, having a try.

But it was no use. The Misses Rostrum assured her, in eager chorus, that Uncle Alvin had not only read it but enjoyed it too.

Barbara sighed and tucked the book under her arm. The Misses Rostrum had lived in her mother's establishment ever since its opening and had come there directly from their father's house across the street after it had been sold at the old man's death. They were thin and gray and elderly and they rarely went out but crept through the halls huddled into hug-me-tights and woolen shawls and spent their time in eating, sleeping, reading aloud to each other, or just sitting. Barbara declared that they reminded her of a couple of dusty old umbrellas, but she admitted, in all justice, that they were sweet old things and always made sure that Uncle Alvin read their library book before it was changed.

Alvin Mott was Mrs. Markham's brother-in-law and occupied a small back room at the top of the house. He had worked all his life for a slender salary at the post office and was now retired on an even more slender pension. I had heard, from Barbara, that he occasionally helped with the housework as part payment for his board.

We changed the book before we had dinner, and Barbara shook her head over the new one. "We shouldn't have been in such a hurry. It's by some doctor—all about the human body—and the poor things don't know they have a body. Nobody ever told them, and I think they shut their eyes when they take a bath, so they won't find out. I hope they don't say anything to Mama—she'll give me the devil."

We got back from the movies at about twelve o'clock and saw that the drawing room was still lighted. We paused in the front hall to shake the snow from our hats, and Barbara whispered, "They're still there. Shall we go in?"

I shook my head regretfully. "We can't. We were paid off for the evening."

"Let's peek then."

She tiptoed over and did a quietly expert job of snooping. I supposed that she had been practicing at those portieres ever since her early childhood. She was back again, almost at once, trying to stifle a series of giggles in her sleeve.

I raised my eyebrows by way of interrogation, and she whispered, "They forgot to pack Camille off to the movies too."

"Camille!" I repeated, appalled.

She was the most frightful bore—an ex-actress in her sixties who continued to bleach her hair, wear high-heeled pumps a full size too small, and short, tight dresses, and who made no bones about admitting that she was nearly forty.

"What's the man like?" I asked.

"Pretty hot, from what I could see of him. Go and take a look."

I went over and peered cautiously through a crack in the portieres. Mary and Grace were looking decidedly bleak and sat grimly silent. A bottle of Mary's best port wine stood on a table and was flanked by three of Mary's fancy crystal wineglasses. Camille, knees crossed, and a lot of stout, champagne-colored leg on exhibition, was drinking some of the wine out of a glass obviously borrowed from the kitchen. She was doing all the talking and was punctuating with hoarse, raucous laughter.

I looked at the man—and I did not need even a second glance. There was no mistaking him. He came direct from Papa's canning factory.

CHAPTER TWO

I FLUNG AWAY and started up the stairs. Barbara followed me and asked curiously, "What's the matter?"

I had to recover my breath on the first landing before I spoke and then I said furiously, "Mary is wasting good port wine, and Camille is wasting her breath. And Grace might just as well be catching a little sleep."

"Why? What are you talking about?"

"That heel down there," I said deliberately, "is going to pay attention to me, and to me only."

"Well, listen to that, will you!" Barbara said, opening her eyes very wide. "You shouldn't be so darned conceited. You're pretty and all that but you can't expect every man to trail you around."

"I know—keep your shirt on. But that man is one of Papa's stooges, and he's been sent here purposely to lure me back to the sticks."

We had reached the second landing, and Miss Imogene must have heard us, for she opened her door and asked us in a whisper if we had her book. Barbara handed it over, and she thanked us effusively and after an exchange of good nights she backed in again and closed the door.

Barbara and I continued up to the third floor where we had adjoining rooms which had been made from one larger room. The partition was thin, and we had placed the heads of our beds against it on each side, so that we could talk back and forth after we were in bed.

I did not want to discuss the man downstairs—I was too angry—but I knew there could be no getting away from it. Barbara would not even talk through the partition but followed me straight into my room. She perched herself on the kitchen chair that had been painted peacock blue and yellow—presumably to disguise it—and said, "Now! Tell me all."

"I told you," I said shortly.

"Don't waste my time, Di. I have to get up earlier in the morning than you do."

"But it makes me mad even to talk about it," I said peevishly. "It's a mean, sneaky thing for Papa to have done, but he'll go to any lengths when he's determined to have his way. You see, he doesn't know that I know this fellow—and I've never actually met him, as far as that goes. But I've seen him twice at the factory and I couldn't mistake him."

"No," Barbara breathed, looking at the wall over my head. "You couldn't exactly mistake him."

"I happened to see him when Papa wasn't with me, both times, and the heel didn't see me because the first time he was talking to one of the bookkeepers and the second time he was talking to the same bookkeeper. She was pretty and had red hair, and he's probably in love with her."

"But your father—"

"You don't know my father," I said crossly. "He once told me I was a sucker for a good-looking man, and it's obvious that he went through his blasted pea factory, picked out the best-looking man, and offered him a raise if he would spend a month in New York making love to me, all expenses paid. Any heel would accept a proposition like that."

"Anybody at all would," Barbara said practically. "He wouldn't have to be a heel."

"I think he would."

"Well, never mind about that. I don't see why you're so mad. You have the jump on them and you've everything to gain and nothing to lose. Go out with him and have yourself a good time. It's your father's money. I only wish—"

"Wait a minute," I said slowly, "maybe that's a good idea. And you can come with us, since Papa's set on throwing his money around."

She said, "Oh no," modestly, but I could see that she liked the idea.

"Grace and Mary too," I said, getting enthusiastic. "I'll tell him I never go anywhere without my girlfriends."

"Now you're getting silly," she said disgustedly and took herself off to bed.

I undressed slowly and when I opened the window before getting into bed I noticed that light was still shining out of the Misses Rostrum's room directly below mine. I decided that they must be getting a kick out of learning about the human body, instead of being offended as Barbara had feared.

The last thing I heard before I dozed off was the sound of Camille's voice saying good night to Papa's stooge on the landing outside my door. Grace and Mary had a couple of larger rooms on the floor below, and Camille must have figured that for once her smaller room on the third floor put her one up on them. I thought drowsily that it was too bad Camille should waste all that sparkle.

I overslept the next morning and missed breakfast altogether. Mrs. Markham closed the dining room at nine o'clock, and when I opened my eyes and saw that it was half past I closed them again and rolled over. In the end I got up in time for lunch, feeling drugged with sleep and having made at least a temporary enemy of Evie. I met her on my way from the bathroom as she was hurrying down stairs to prepare for her job as waitress, and she flung over her shoulder, "I don't know when I'll be able to get your room done, miss."

I decided without interest that it would mean an extra tip—and then I remembered Papa's obstinacy and realized that she'd be lucky to get the usual minimum. So I made my own bed and tidied up the room instead.

I was the first one into the dining room but I was closely followed by Imogene and Opal Rostrum, and Barbara's uncle, Alvin Mott. They were always punctual, I suppose because meals meant a break in the monotony and were important.

Camille shuffled around in the doorway until Papa's stooge appeared, and then she made an entrance with him, talking animatedly. He had a small table to himself, but Camille was seated close enough to spray him with bright talk and raucous laughter. I kept my head turned away in perverse determination to make it as hard as possible for the heel to scrape an acquaintance with me.

Miss Giddens wandered in next and doddered to her table in a far, dark corner of the room. I don't know how old she was, but she looked to be about a hundred, and nobody paid much attention to her. She was seated apart because her table manners were pretty bad.

Mr. Neville Ward made his appearance exactly ten minutes after the gong had sounded, as was his invariable custom. He worked in a bank near by and was a bachelor of the old-maid type, intensely respectable and about as exciting as a boiled egg. Grace and Mary often used him when they needed an escort.

I sat at a table with Mrs. Markham and Barbara—a distinct concession from Mrs. Markham, since she and her daughter had always had an inconspicuous table to themselves, but Barbara had fought for me and was given her way in the end.

I was halfway through the meal when they came in. Mrs. Markham gave her usual quick look around to see who was there and sat down with a barely perceptible nod of satisfaction. She hated people to be late for meals, and everyone was there except Grace and Mary, who never came back for lunch.

"I suppose you girls will be striking attitudes in the drawing room all afternoon," she said cheerily.

"Not all afternoon, Mama," Barbara said. "We can have one session while they're all taking their afternoon naps and then another session when they go back up to change for dinner."

"That'll be nice," Mrs. Markham said absently, and I could see that her energetic mind had already passed on to some housekeeping problem. She was a small, brisk woman with cool, pale blue eyes, and smooth gray hair.

Barbara and I went to the drawing room directly after lunch and waited quietly for the room to empty. Miss Giddens had disappeared like a silent, wrinkled old ghost, and Neville Ward smoked a cigarette without once dropping ash anywhere except into the ashtray and then went off to his bank. Alvin Mott retired to his room for a nap, but the Misses Rostrum sat side by side on their favorite couch and told Barbara and me how very much they were enjoying the library book we had brought them.

Papa's stooge appeared presently with Camille still telling him all about it. He got Camille to introduce him to Barbara and me, and his name turned out to be Dennis Livingstone. I curled my lips at him until Barbara nudged me and then I remembered our plan to exploit him and Papa, and relaxed.

However, when the two Rostrums left to take their naps I nudged Barbara, and we left too. "He'd only hang around as long as I stayed," I explained, "and Camille would hang around as long as he stayed. Maybe they'll go away now, and we can sneak back and have the drawing room to ourselves."

We waited in the back hall for some time, but they did not leave, and after a while Miss Giddens appeared from nowhere and shrilly demanded to know what we were doing skulking around the house like this. We fled then and did our stuff as well as we could in my bedroom. We stayed there until five-thirty, when we tried the drawing room again, and finding it empty, had a good rehearsal until the gong sounded for dinner.

We discovered that Grace and Mary had Dennis Livingstone at their table. I knew they thought they had played a master stroke and I shook my head over the waste of strategy.

The Misses Rostrum chose that evening to break the habit of a lifetime and gravely displeased Mrs. Markham by fluttering in to dinner when everyone else was finishing. They knew they were in the doghouse and they crept up to our table and timidly apologized. "We were so interested in our conversation," Imogene explained meekly, "that I guess we forgot the time."

"Didn't you hear the gong?" Mrs. Markham asked with a bright smile and a layer of frost sparkling in her pale eyes.

"No, I guess we never noticed it," Opal chirped.

We left just as they were starting on the soup—but we never got as far as the drawing room. Mary stopped us in the hall and asked, "You girls going to the movies tonight?"

Barbara and I didn't bother to answer. We merely extended our hands, and Mary put exactly forty cents into each palm with the remark that the best program was the one around the corner.

She went off, and Barbara and I giggled. "Shall we go?" I asked.

"Sure. We can get back early, and maybe he'll take us to a night club."

We got into our hats and coats, and then Barbara decided to see if the Rostrums had finished their book. "It'll save me a trip tomorrow if I change it tonight," she explained.

We found Imogene and Opal in the dining room, making their way through the boiled lamb. They both looked up as we entered, and Barbara asked about the book.

Miss Imogene opened her mouth to reply, but no words came, and the mouth remained hanging open. I looked at her in astonishment and saw that she was staring at Barbara with eyes like china saucers. Miss Opal glanced in bewilderment at her sister and then looked at Barbara—and suddenly she was on her feet, while her fork made a sharp clatter as it dropped to the floor.

CHAPTER THREE

"WHAT'S THE MATTER?" Barbara asked with a shade of irritation.

Miss Imogene recovered herself and murmured, "Oh, nothing—nothing, dear."

They resumed their seats, and Miss Opal said confusedly, "We—we've finished the book."

"Then you want me to change it, don't you?" Barbara asked briskly. "I don't think Uncle Alvin would care for it."

"No, wait—he does—he said he wanted to read it."

Miss Imogene appeared to be thoroughly discomposed, and Miss Opal lowered her eyes and began to worry her food in a distracted manner.

Barbara took a long breath, probably counted ten, and said agreeably, "Then I'll leave it until he has finished with it."

"Yes—yes, if you will, dear," Miss Imogene murmured.

We were quiet until we got outside the front door, and then Barbara gave an exasperated laugh. "What in the world was the matter with them? They stared at me as though I'd put a beard on or something."

"Probably your lipstick. You have too much on."

"They don't object to lipstick, for heaven's sake. Miss Opal once told me that if their father had only allowed them to use makeup she was pretty sure they would have been able to get married."

A thaw had set in, and the snow had disappeared in a dribble of slush. We made our way along the drying sidewalks and had almost reached the theater when I discovered that I had forgotten my purse.

"We'll have to go back," I said. "I don't know where I left it, but it has money in it, and I can't afford to lose any."

Barbara turned back resignedly, and we presently slipped quietly through the front door and into the hall again.

"It can't be in the drawing room," I said, glancing at the drawn portieres. "I haven't been in there since dinner and I certainly had it with me during dinner."

Barbara followed my glance and whispered, "Let's peek and see how things are going."

The situation appeared to be considerably improved. Camille was not in evidence, and Mary, Grace, Neville, and Dennis were playing bridge. Alvin was sitting in a corner, apparently staring at them, and Mrs. Markham was in an armchair near by, her small hands busy with some knitting.

Barbara let the heavy drapes fall back into position and whispered, "I wonder what they've done with Camille?"

"She's probably lying in her room bound and gagged."

"Well, come on, let's look in the dining room. You probably left your purse there."

The dining room was still lighted. The Misses Rostrum had gone, but their places had not been cleared, and Barbara shook her head. "I suppose Evie and Kate are having dinner, but Mama will be furious if she sees this. They are not supposed to eat until the dining room has been cleared and put in order."

I glanced at the plates and said curiously, "Look—the Rostrum gals never ate another bite after we left. And they love their food dearly too. I wonder what they had on their minds."

"They should have their heads X-rayed," Barbara said impatiently. "I've thought so for some time. There's your purse, on the table."

We made the movies without mishap that time and when we returned we went straight into the drawing room, because Barbara declared that there was no use pussyfooting any longer and we might as well start getting whatever gravy Dennis was prepared to dish out.

The bridge game was still going on and had become quite gay, and the players up to and including Papa's stooge gave us four brief nods and returned to their fun. There was a fresh bottle of wine—not Mary's, this time—and an expensive-looking bottle of scotch, and glasses all over the place. Uncle Alvin and Mrs. Markham apparently had gone to bed, and Camille was still mysteriously missing.

Barbara and I retired to a couch and lighted cigarettes. "He has a nerve," she whispered to me, "spending money on Grace and Mary that he should be saving for you."

"I don't care. I love to see Papa's money going to waste."

"But we're not getting much fun out of this," Barbara said discontentedly. "He hasn't even offered us a drink."

Nor did he. The man actually ignored us. In fact, we were ignored altogether, except for Grace, who gave us a meaning frown. She meant, of course, that we were cheating but, as Barbara said later, she could hardly expect the same value for a forty-cent movie as she had received for dinner and a downtown movie.

However, we rose and left because it seemed pretty obvious that we were not wanted by anyone. Neville had never liked us and said good night stiffly. Mary and Grace were charming, and Dennis casual, as though we were the Misses Rostrum. In fact, we felt a bit like the Misses Rostrum when we got out into the hall.

"There must be some mistake," Barbara declared. "That man's not trying to make up to you. It must be someone else."

"Oh no, it isn't. He's playing some sort of a game, that's all."

Barbara yawned and shook her head. "I think you're all balled up. Anyway, let's go to bed."

On the second floor we ran into Miss Giddens in her nightgown. "I can't sleep," she announced, giving us a severe look.

Barbara assumed the voice that she had learned to use on the inmates. "That's too bad, Miss Giddens."

"I dropped it out the window," the old lady said crossly. "Right out the window."

"What did you drop out the window?"

"My shawl. It fell right out."

"We'll get it for you in the morning," Barbara said with a bright smile and made a move to pass on.

Miss Giddens caught at her sleeve. "I'm cold—the house is very cold—and I want my shawl."

"Haven't you another shawl you could wear, just for tonight?" Barbara said persuasively. "And then, in the morning—"

"No, no, no—they'll steal it—they're down there right now." She started to shamble toward the stairs. "Hurry—must hurry."

Barbara caught at the old lady's shoulder and began to urge her toward her room. "All right," she said, hanging on to her temper, "you go on back to bed now, and I'll bring your shawl right up to you."

Miss Giddens allowed herself to be led back to her room, but at the door she turned around and peered up at Barbara anxiously. "You must get my shawl at once," she said distinctly, "before they bury it."

I went downstairs with Barbara and asked curiously, "What does she mean? Who'd want to bury her shawl?"

"She's crazy," Barbara said impatiently. "She doesn't know what she's talking about half the time."

"Maybe she didn't drop her shawl out the window then."

"Oh, I guess she did. She's always dropping things out. Mama's been thinking of having the window barred in case she accidentally drops herself out sometime."

Down in the front hall we could hear shrieks of laughter coming from the drawing room, and even Neville's voice could be heard with the rest. I believe it was the first time I had ever heard Neville laugh.

Barbara and I stared at each other. "Pretty nice going," she said, cocking an eyebrow. "Maybe when we get to be thirty we'll know a little more about technique."

"I know you have to do something pretty drastic to get rid of Camille," I said, shaking my head. "But I don't think they should have murdered her."

Barbara giggled. "Camille's on one of her periodic disappearances. She stays in her room for several days, every once in a while, and explains that she's subject to migraine. Actually, she holes in to do some real drinking."

"If she must go on a bat periodically why doesn't she do it in the open where she'd have more fun?" I asked sensibly.

"She's very careful about drinking in public," Barbara said. "She'll never take anything more than a little wine."

"Doesn't she know that dates her?" I asked idly.

Barbara had switched on the light in the kitchen and was struggling with the bolt on the back door. "The damn thing needs oil," she muttered and gave a terrific heave. The bolt gave, then, with a screech that put my teeth on edge.

We went down the steps into the small back yard. "I used to play here," Barbara said, "when I was a little girl. But now the only reason I ever come here is to pick up something the old imbecile has dropped out of her window."

It was very dark, and I could not see anything, but Barbara made straight for a spot that apparently was directly under Miss Giddens' window. I followed gingerly, but though the two of us scoured the ground for some distance around we could not find a sign of any shawl. We began to shiver after a while, and I remembered that we had left our coats in the front hall.

"Come on," I said, hugging myself with my arms, "the poor old thing's made some sort of a mistake, and I'm cold."

We turned toward the steps, and at the same moment someone closed the back door, and we could hear the squeaky bolt shoot home.

"For heaven's sake, who's locking us out?" Barbara said shrilly.

"Somebody found the door open, and of course they didn't know we were out here. Come on, I'm freezing. We'll have to go around to the front."

We altered our course and made for the side of the house.

Our eyes had become better accustomed to the darkness by that time, and Barbara stopped with a sudden exclamation. "Look. There's the wretched shawl, over there."

I turned my head and could see a patch of white on the ground, farther down the yard.

Barbara started toward it, and I followed, several steps behind. And then, quite suddenly and without a sound, she disappeared completely.

CHAPTER FOUR

I STOOD QUITE STILL, my eyes straining into the darkness and my heart pumping madly. I began to have a queer, wild feeling that I was dreaming, and then I heard a groan, followed by a string of wicked oaths. There was no mistaking Barbara's brand of swearing, and relief flooded through me coolly. I took a cautious forward step and saw her.

She was struggling out of a large hole in the ground, and I leaned over and helped her. At the side on which we stood the excavation was something over a foot deep, but it appeared to be graduated on the other side. The whole thing was in the shape of a large square.

"It's Mama's tulip bed," Barbara explained, trying to brush bits of earth and dead leaves from her sweater. "I thought the damned bulbs had been put in weeks ago."

"You don't have to dig a ditch like this for tulips."

"Uncle Alvin does the gardening," Barbara said without interest. "Mama tells him what she wants done. Maybe he's transplanting a tree or something. Anyway, I don't care if he's merely trying to get through to China—I've hurt my ankle and I'm frozen through to the bone. Go and get the shawl, will you? And let's get back into the house."

I skirted the ditch and halfway around I stumbled over a shovel. "You'd think he'd have the common decency to put his tools away," I said crossly. But Barbara was already making for the house, so I picked up the shawl, which was lying near the shovel, and raced after her.

When we reached the front door we realized that we had no keys, and Barbara said, "I suppose everyone's in bed except the bunch in the drawing room. We'd better not ring. Let's bang on the window and get one of them to let us in."

It took a great deal of banging to raise anyone, but at last, after we had nearly smashed the window Dennis loomed up behind the curtain and peered out. Barbara made frantic signs toward the front door, and Dennis elevated his eyebrows and disappeared again. We shifted over to the door and when Dennis opened it we slid in. We were shivering violently, and Barbara was messed up with bits of earth and twigs and dead leaves.

Dennis looked us over. "Been for a stroll?" he asked.

"Just down to the Battery and back," I said between my banging teeth.

"Good thing you took a wrap along," he observed, glancing at the soiled, shabby old shawl. "The nights are getting a trifle chilly."

I hastily passed the shawl to Barbara, and he turned to her. "Did you get run down by a truck?"

Barbara, trying to fold the grimy shawl into as small a bundle as possible, said yes, but she had decided not to sue.

Mary appeared just then and said, "I thought it sounded like the high-school kids." She was smiling, but Barbara and I immediately said good night and started for the stairs, Barbara limping a trifle.

Dennis said, "Just a minute. You girls had better have a drink. You seem to be chilled through."

Barbara and I turned with one accord and looked at Mary, and she said resignedly, "I guess you'd better—you look fit to come down with pneumonia. Where the devil have you been, anyway?"

We edged into the drawing room without answering, and Dennis poured some scotch.

Neville gave us a pale stare and asked fussily, "Do you think your mother would approve your drinking scotch, Barbara?"

"Oh yes," Barbara said easily. "In fact, she always insists."

"Where have you two been?" Grace demanded.

Barbara explained and finished by asking, "Who locked us out?"

"Don't look at us," Mary said, shrugging. "We've all been playing here for the past hour or two."

"I went to the kitchen for some ice a little while ago," Dennis admitted, "but I remember very clearly that I did not lock the door on you."

The conversation became general after that, and what with everyone trying to say something smart and witty, I got a bit sleepy and lost most of the threads.

Dennis' voice brought me back with a jerk after a while. He was saying, ". . . an old fool who runs a canning factory. Quincy Prescott. Silly name, isn't it?"

I sat up with my eyes blazing and saw that Dennis was looking at me expectantly. I closed my teeth over the words I had been about to pour out and took time to wonder what his little game was. I relaxed back into my chair and said as calmly as I could, "He may be an old fool in some ways, but Quincy knows how to get peas into cans like nobody's business. And he could buy and sell you several times over."

"Oh, undoubtedly," Dennis agreed. "You know Quincy, then?"

"Don't be a silly fool," I said with some heat. "I know why you're here, and I know you know I know Quincy."

"Can't you make that clearer?" asked Dennis.

"Never mind," I said, getting to my feet. "Let's all go out tomorrow night, all of us. We'll do a show and a night club, and you can foot the bill."

"I?"

"Don't refuse," I cut in, "or I'll write to Quincy and tell him I'm sitting home each night while you gad around with other girls."

"So far from refusing," said Dennis with a lot of dignity, "I was about to ask you what play you wished us all to see."

"Settle it among yourselves," I said handsomely and made my way out of the room.

I went up the stairs and on the second floor I found Miss Giddens wandering around, either again, or still. She shuffled over to me and whispered, "Did you get it?"

"Oh, I'm sorry," I murmured, remembering the shawl. "Barbara has it. I guess she'll bring it right up."

"Did she bury it?"

"No," I said impatiently. "She is going to bring it to you."

She moved away from me with a satisfied nod. "Good—that's good! When I saw her pick it up I thought she was going to bury it, you know. But I'll wait here—I'll wait right here till Barbara comes with my shawl."

I went on upstairs accompanied by a guilty feeling that I ought to go down again and get the poor thing's shawl for her.

When I reached the third floor Mrs. Markham opened her door and peered out. She wore a neat flannel robe and woolly slippers, and her bang was done up in curlers.

"Is Barbara in?" she asked anxiously.

"She's downstairs in the drawing room with some of the others, Mrs. Markham."

"Oh, that's all right then," she said in a relieved voice. "I had not heard her come in and I knew you had both gone to the movies. It's getting so late that I was beginning to be uneasy."

We said good night, and she closed her door while I went on to my room.

They must have had quite a party in the drawing room that night because I woke up at five o'clock and heard Barbara sneaking into bed.

I had to attend classes that day and did not get back to the house until four in the afternoon. The drawing room seemed to be deserted, so I went in, hoping that Barbara would show up and that we could get an hour's work together. I sat down to wait and discovered immediately that I was not alone. Dennis had been there all the time, more or less wrapped around by a wing chair.

"Hello," he said amiably.

I nodded stiffly.

"Where have you been keeping yourself? I've looked high and low for you."

"If you were really on the job and worth your salary," I said scornfully, "you'd have been up in time to carry my books to school for me."

"I was up at eight-fifteen on the dot," he said mildly, "and busy as a beaver all day—trying to cross your path."

"Save it for your expense account. Did you get those tickets?"

"I got tickets for the most popular show in town, for you and me."

"You and me?" I repeated indignantly. "What about the rest of them?"

He shook his head. "Sorry, I can't do it. I phoned the old man, and he said in more words than a few that it was to be you and you alone."

"Then you'd better phone him right back," I said furiously, "and resign. Because I won't go anywhere without my girlfriends, and that includes Neville too."

He laughed heartily, and I bounced out of my chair and went over to the window where I stared out and made a little fog on the pane because I was breathing so quickly.

Mary and Grace came up the front steps as I stood there and gave me a couple of cheerful smiles. I turned away and found Dennis directly behind me.

"Won't you reconsider, about that show?" he asked persuasively. "The old man will make biting comment if he finds out that I haven't managed a date with you yet."

"Frankly," I said, "I don't care."

"Obviously—but it's a pity to waste the tickets. If I can't persuade you to go with me won't you accept a ticket and go by yourself? Of course you'll find me sitting beside you when you get there, but then you're apt to rub shoulders with all kinds at these public places."

I wanted to see the show and I began to waver, but I had one more try first. "Give me both tickets," I suggested, "and I'll take Barbara."

He said, "No. I don't very often get a chance to do the New York theaters."

"All right," I muttered through my teeth. "Give me the ticket."

He handed it over as Grace and Mary walked into the room. There was a fusillade of loud and cheery greetings, and I slipped out and left them to it.

I met Barbara hurrying toward the stairs from the back regions. "Have to get dressed," she said, rushing past me. "Got a decent date."

"Who is it?" I asked, following upstairs.

"Tom," she called over her shoulder. "Show, dancing, dinner—all the trimmings . . ." She said something more which I did not hear because she had got so far ahead of me. She was halfway up the stairs to the third floor by the time I had reached the second-floor landing.

Mrs. Markham was coming out of the Misses Rostrum's room, and she stopped me with a quick little gesture. Her brows were drawn together in a worried frown, and she came over and said in an agitated whisper, "I don't know what to do. Miss Imogene and Miss Opal have completely disappeared."

CHAPTER FIVE

I STARED AT HER and repeated foolishly.

"Disappeared?"

She was wearing a dull green knitted dress and she began to worry the tassels that hung from the neck. "My dear, I don't know what to think. Evie says their beds were made this morning, although they sometimes do that themselves. But they did not appear at breakfast and they're not here now. You know they never go anywhere—except, perhaps, once in three or four months—and then they get all excited about it for weeks in advance."

"Well, I don't know," I said uncertainly. "Maybe they received a telegram from a relative or something."

Mrs. Markham shook her head in a dissatisfied manner.

"If they had they'd have fainted first and then come to me to make all their arrangements."

"Have you asked the other guests if they know anything?"

"No, but I'll attend to it at once." She smoothed the knitted dress over her small hips and went briskly down the stairs as though she were relieved by having something definite to do.

I made my way to the third floor, and as I stepped onto the landing Camille poked her head out of her door and said huskily, "Do come in for a minute."

I detoured reluctantly and entered the small, stuffy, untidy room. Camille was wound up in a soiled blue satin wrapper, and her bleached, streaky hair hung around her face in dry snarls. The room was littered with clothes and messy ashtrays, and the top of the bureau looked like a cut-rate cosmetic counter.

She carelessly removed a rubble of underwear from the chair and asked me to sit down. I perched myself gingerly, while she climbed back into bed. She was sniffling damply and appeared to have a bad cold.

"I've been very ill," she said pathetically, "and not a soul has come near me. Not even Opal or Imogene, and they always come to see when I'm laid on my back."

"I'm sorry," I said uncomfortably.

"Even Alvin—I think somebody must have been getting at him. You'd certainly think he'd come to see me, being the way he is about me, the poor old droop."

"How is he about you?" I asked, trying to look innocent.

"Haven't you noticed?" she yelled. "Why, he's crazy about me."

I hadn't noticed. As far as I could see Alvin went on eating and sleeping, dressing and undressing simply because his parents had called him into being. He didn't appear to be crazy about anything.

Camille blew her nose and croaked, "My dear, he's been silently adoring me for years, even before he married Lulu's sister."

"Lulu?"

"Mrs. Markham."

"Oh, of course," I said, nodding.

"I was only a child at the time," Camille explained hastily. "But even so . . . And then I went on the stage. I'd have been an outstanding success, except that I allowed my heart to rule my head. I married three times, and marriage certainly pulls you down. If you want some really good advice, my dear—*don't* get married."

"I will too," I said, feeling antagonized for no particular reason.

She blew her nose again and looked offended. "Some people," she observed, "can learn only through experience."

I managed to get away then and after I had taken several long breaths of the more or less fresh air in the hall I went along to Barbara's room to see if I could lend a helping hand.

She had my silver-fox coat on the bed, and my new red satin shoes on her feet, and appeared to be almost ready. "I had to borrow a pair of your stockings," she informed me carelessly.

"That's the last straw," I said, sitting on the bed and resting my arms on the footboard while I watched her putting on the finishing touches.

"What's the time?"

"It's only five-thirty," I said, glancing at my watch.

"Well, he's coming for me at six. God! These shoes hurt. Why do you get them so small ?"

"Damn it," I said in exasperation, "they're the size of my feet."

"I don't believe it." She put her hand mirror back onto the bureau and began very carefully to slip her dress over her head. She said something more, which was muffed in the folds of the dress.

I buttoned her up and asked mildly, "Do you think silver fox suits this costume?"

"Sure. Why? Do you think your mink would be better?"

"No," I said and gave up.

There was a tap at the door, and Uncle Alvin stuck his head in. "Your mother wants to see you before you go, Barbara."

"Why?" she asked impatiently.

"It's about Imogene and Opal. Do you know where they are?"

"Lord, no," Barbara said. She was carefully painting her nails and she added, without looking up, "Maybe somebody took 'em out to the park on a leash. Tell Mama I'm late. I'll try and see her before I go but I don't know whether I can make it or not."

Uncle Alvin started to shuffle off, and I asked politely, "Did you get your tulips in?"

He paused, looked at me vaguely, and repeated, "Tulips?"

"Bulbs," I said, wishing I'd never started it. "Don't you plant them in the fall?"

His face lighted up, "Oh yes—yes. I always get them in before the end of October. Put them in with a little sand."

Barbara interrupted him. "In that case, someone's dug them up again. There's a big hole in the bed."

To my utter astonishment, Uncle Alvin went off into a rage, a thing I would not have supposed him capable of doing. He made some opprobrious remarks about certain neighbors who were not above bulb stealing and rushed away, presumably to look into it.

Barbara laughed and observed without much interest, "Uncle Alvin certainly loves his garden."

She gave herself a last look in the mirror and, picking up my coat—carefully, because the lacquer on her nails was not dry—started downstairs. I followed with the idea of standing on the drawing-room side of the black portieres and having a look at this Tom when he came in. I figured I might be able to tell whether Barbara was in love with him by the way they greeted each other.

However, he was already in the hall when we got down, so Barbara had to introduce me. I asked him how he did, inquired about the state of the weather, and then faded away. I sidled through the portieres and put my eye to the slit, as Barbara had taught me.

They kissed lightly—Tom asked her if she still loved him, and she said, "madly"—after which he produced a box. The box yielded up an orchid—not a white orchid but an orchid orchid. I groaned, and so did Barbara, because the red shoes and the orchid orchid made even the fox coat look, somehow, as though it had been borrowed from Camille.

Tom looked at her anxiously and asked if anything were wrong.

"Not a thing," Barbara declared bravely. "I always groan when I get orchids. They're so beautiful, it hurts."

That seemed to settle Tom. He brightened up and proudly helped her to pin the thing on. As they turned to go Barbara glanced at the portieres and said, " 'By, Diana."

I backed away in confusion and felt my face glowing, but there was worse to come. I turned around and was confronted by a row of curious faces. Grace, Neville, Miss Giddens, Camille, and Dennis were sitting about on various chairs, and not one of them had made a sound.

Dennis broke the silence. "Is it worth getting up for?" he asked politely.

"It was," I said, wishing my face would cool off. "But it's all over."

Neville murmured, "Disgraceful!" without quite looking at me.

Miss Giddens padded over to the portieres and had a look for herself.

I swallowed a couple of times and nonchalantly asked Grace for a cigarette. Dennis supplied me, and Camille told him she'd have one too.

"How's your cold?" I asked her, not caring in the least, but still seeking *savoir-faire.*

"It's very bad, but I can't stay in my room another minute. I get so lonely."

"You should have the doctor," Neville said fussily. "it's madness to neglect a cold. They so often lead to pneumonia."

Mary stuck her head through the portieres and, without saying a word, got Grace's attention, and managed to convey that there were cocktails. Grace immediately did a neat job of plucking Dennis from Camille and marching him out of the room. I followed close behind them and I don't believe the three of them noticed me at all until Mary absently handed me a cocktail and then actually saw me for the first time.

I took the cocktail quickly, and she said, "How the devil did you get here?"

"I hopped a cab," I said, hanging on to the stem of the glass firmly.

She murmured, "Shut up!" and gave her attention to Grace, who was saying, "Have you heard about the Rostrums? They seem to have disappeared off the face of the earth, and Mrs. Markham has half a mind to call in the police."

Dennis said, "They'll probably show up again," and Mary added, "You never know what the poor old creatures are up to half the time."

The cocktails were a success. We had so much fun, in the end, that Mary went so far as to forgive me for crashing her party.

Both Mary and Grace seemed to know why Dennis was in New York, and it turned out that Barbara had spilled it all to them. They thought it was a great joke.

"I wish I had a father who was thoughtful enough to arrange a marriage for me with the handsomest man he could find," Grace said with a loud sigh.

I stared at Dennis and said, "Handsome?"

Mary told me not to be an ass. "He's the best-looking piece I've ever seen," she declared emphatically.

"You can't dispute it," Dennis said to me reasonably.

"What else have you?" I asked.

"Nothing," he admitted amiably, "but what else do I need? Look at me now. All play and no work—expenses paid—and nothing to do but make up to the boss's daughter."

Grace was closing out on her fourth cocktail, and she shook her head sadly. "I don't believe you should have accepted that job. It's not quite a he-man's occupation."

Mary said, "Personally, I don't like he-men."

Dennis said he didn't, either, and added that they smelled of horses and tobacco.

This sent Grace off into gales of hysterical laughter, and by the time we got her straightened out Evie was knocking on the door and announcing, in an aggrieved voice, that dinner was almost over.

We herded down, and I sat at my table alone, since Mrs. Markham had finished. I was glad to postpone meeting her eye because I knew we were all in the doghouse.

It was almost eight o'clock before we had finished, and Dennis paused by my table on his way out to say, "Better hurry—show starts at eight-thirty."

I flew upstairs and washed up and then hurried down again. Dennis was nowhere to be seen, so I took a cab and went by myself.

To my surprise and growing annoyance, Dennis never did show up. The seat beside me remained vacant throughout the performance, and I was angry at the stupid waste. There were so many people who would have enjoyed that seat—Camille—or any of them at the house.

I came directly home from the theater and got in at a little before twelve. A dim light burned in the hall in a surrounding cavern of blackness—and yet I saw it at once.

The black portieres were gone.

CHAPTER SIX

I STARED AT THE BLANK, yawning archway for a moment and then shook myself and decided that Mrs. Markham had taken the portiers down to have them cleaned. I wondered idly who had selected black as a color: it seemed unnecessarily depressing.

I remained there for a while in the absolute stillness, looking into the dark drawing room and wondering where Grace and Mary and Dennis had betaken themselves—and as I looked the shadows stirred, and a dim, white figure detached itself and moved silently toward me.

I recognized Miss Giddens, in her nightgown, before I fainted and so saved myself the embarrassment. She wore nothing over the nightgown, and in the reaction from shock I scolded her rather sharply.

"Why aren't you in bed?" I demanded. "Running around like that— you'll get pneumonia."

She peered at me and said, "Yes—but I have lost my shawl."

"I'm not going out to the yard to look for it tonight," I declared firmly. "You'll have to wrap up in something else."

She asked mildly, "Where's Barbara?"

"She's out—and she won't be back until late. You'd better come to bed." I took her arm and began to urge her toward the stairs. She allowed me to lead her across the hall but at the foot of the stairs she stopped, shook her head, and refused to go further. I could feel her shivering through the soiled old flannel nightgown.

"What's the matter?" I asked, trying to be patient. "Don't you want to get into bed, where you'll be warm and comfortable?"

She appeared to think it over and finally nodded. "Yes," she said.

"Then why won't you let me help you upstairs?" I pulled gently at her arm, but she refused to budge.

"No. I don't like that woman."

"What woman?"

"I told her to go away," said Miss Giddens, "but she wouldn't. It's my room, you know—it has always been any room."

"I'm afraid I don't know what you're talking about," I said, still polite.

She blinked at me owlishly and said nothing.

I tried again. "Where is this woman? In your room?"

She nodded. "In my room—yes. And of course it's my room."

I agreed heartily. "Certainly it's your room. And I'm sure that woman has gone away now. You come on up and get to bed where you'll be warm. She won't bother you again."

Miss Giddens fastened her beady little black eyes on my face. "Did you tell her she must get out?"

"Yes," I lied. "I told her to go, and she went. So now you can go to bed."

She started up without another word, at that, and disappeared onto the second floor with surprising speed.

I was wide awake and hungry and I decided to find out if Mrs. Markham locked up the groceries when they were not in use. I went through the back hall to the dining room and from there into the vast serving pantry. It was in darkness, but there was a glow along the bottom of the door leading to the kitchen, and I swung it open a crack and peeped in.

Dennis was seated at the kitchen table, gnawing on a beef bone.

I pushed the door wide and went in. "I suppose you know that's tomorrow's lunch you're working on."

He stood up with the bone in his hand and said courteously, "Please sit down and share tomorrow's lunch with me."

I glanced at the table and saw milk, bread, butter, and marmalade, so I sat down. I left Dennis in possession of the bone and got to work on the bread and butter and marmalade.

He resumed his chair and observed, "Don't let tomorrow's lunch upset you. I intend to leave some of your father's money on the table when I depart."

"Leave two dollars," I said promptly, "and then I can take one. God knows I need it."

"Taking subject to supper, two dollars," he said reflectively. "No, that would be cheating the boss, and I've always been honest. Honesty—"

"Never mind," I sighed. "If you're not going to give me the dollar, don't—but you needn't say it with flowers."

"I suppose I could give you five," he said, "but it would have to go down on the expense account. Five dollars borrowed by subject."

I extended my hand and said, "Good! You couldn't make it ten, could you?"

"No," said Dennis, "I couldn't."

He watched me put the bill in my purse and then asked, "How did you enjoy the show?"

"Very much. You should see it sometime."

"I shall. Unfortunately, something turned up tonight to prevent my going."

"How do you put that down?" I asked. "Forced to let subject attend theater alone, owing to pressing business at cocktail party with brunette?"

He laughed. "I'm going to leave that item out. The boss will never know unless you inform on me, and if you do I'll be fired, and then you won't be able to borrow a fiver when you need it."

"I won't inform on you. Where are you taking me tomorrow night?"

Dennis placed the bone firmly on the table and stared at me. "Do you mean that I'm making progress after all?"

"The whole idea made me mad at first," I explained, "but I've changed my mind. I might just as well go around with you and take what fun there is to be had out of it until Papa catches on that it's doing him no good."

Dennis began to clean up the outlying bits of beef from himself and the table with a napkin. "Very sensible attitude—and of course it means something to me. I'll be made general manager."

"General manager!" I repeated, opening my eyes very wide. "But what about old Casey?"

"He's retiring," Dennis said carelessly. "My being general manager depends upon whether I marry you. If I get you home without marrying you it will be considered good work—but not necessarily permanent—and will mean, I believe, assistant to the general manager. If I fail to move, in any way, your desire to be an actress I shall be demoted to assistant to myself."

"What do you mean?"

"Well, you see," he explained, "your father will put the word 'assistant' in front of my present title. He won't put anyone over me or change the job in any other way—he's too smart. My punishment will be a loss of face."

"Why, I think that's terrible!" I said hotly. "Who does he think he is! Tampering with the lives of his employees like that!"

"Ah, well," said Dennis, shrugging, "come the revolution, all will be changed. Your old man will be digging ditches."

I shook my head. "I guess you don't know Papa very well. He'll be down in Washington with 'Commissar Prescott' on his office door."

Dennis laughed for some time at that until a muffled thud, apparently from the front of the house somewhere, stopped him.

"What was that?" he asked abruptly.

"I guess somebody dropped something," I said, frowning. "I hope it wasn't Miss Giddens dropping herself instead of her shawl."

"Perhaps we'd better go and see." He stood up, and I followed him out of the kitchen and along the front hall.

The dim light was still burning, and everything was quiet and apparently in order. The archway to the drawing room yawned emptily.

"What happened to the portieres?" I asked, almost whispering.

Dennis glanced at the drawing room. "I don't know. They were in place when I left and gone when I returned. It's going to make things a bit difficult for you."

"Why?"

"No more peeping."

I blushed and hastily started up the stairs to hide it.

Dennis followed me, and just as we reached the first landing the front door opened and Barbara came in. I stopped and leaned over the balustrade and after a moment I found Dennis beside me, offering his cigarette case. "Might as well have one," he said in a low voice. "It may take them some time to say good night, and we don't want to miss anything."

I helped myself in silence and arranged my arms comfortably on the railing, but the goodnight scene was a washout. Barbara shook hands with Tom; he bowed formally and left, and she started up the stairs, carelessly swinging my silver-fox coat in one hand. I noticed that the orchid had disappeared and assumed that she had conveniently lost it.

"Aren't you going to skip before you're discovered?" Dennis whispered.

I said, "No, I'm the honest type."

Barbara looked up and said, "Hello."

"What happened?" I asked. "You were definitely cold to him."

"The stuffed shirt," she said disgustedly. "He insisted that we had to get home early on account of he's a businessman, and he doesn't want to jeopardize his career by too much play."

I whistled, and Dennis asked, "What do you girls expect, anyway?"

"And your shoes are killing me," Barbara went on, "and he danced all over the parts that hurt most."

We went on up to the third floor, and Barbara announced, "I get the bathroom first because of my feet killing me."

"Fair enough," Dennis agreed. "I'll toss with Diana for second."

"No, you won't," I said. "You can have second. I'm having a long hot bath and I don't want to be hurried."

"At this time of night?" Barbara yawned.

I glanced at my watch and saw that it was after one. "Oh, well—I don't have to get up in the morning."

We said goodnight and retired to our rooms. I undressed slowly while Barbara kept up a running stream of description, through the partition, about the night's doings. Sometimes I listened and sometimes not. She settled into silence after a while, and I went out to take my bath.

In the hall I was startled by the sound of footsteps and turned to find Miss Giddens climbing the stairs. I expelled a loud, exasperated breath, and she looked up at me as she made the last step. "Good morning," she said courteously.

"It's not morning," I said, trying not to be cross. "Go back to bed, Miss Giddens, or you'll certainly have a cold."

"I can't sleep—I can't sleep at all with that woman there. I don't like her."

"What woman?" I asked and wondered why I wasted my breath.

She made no answer and stood looking vaguely around the hall.

"Come on," I said resignedly, "I'll go to your room with you and get the woman out of there so that you can sleep."

Her eyes focused on me again, and she said, "It's very kind of you, very kind. It's my room, you know."

She padded down the stairs beside me and then hung back while I went ahead into the room. It was quite large and was solidly jammed with furniture both good and bad. I glanced around, and then Miss Giddens pressed up behind me and pointed a bony old finger at the floor behind the door.

I looked down and felt a chill seep along my spine. A dark, tumbled mass of plush lay at my feet, and I recognized one of the black portieres. I stooped over and pulled at the material with a shaking hand—and looked straight into a dead, blue, contorted mass of features. Only the hair and dress told me that it was Opal Rostrum.

CHAPTER SEVEN

I STUMBLED BACK and screamed sharply, twice. Miss Giddens was clinging to my arm, and she began to whimper like a small child.

I backed into the hall and became conscious of Mary's firm hand on my shoulder. "What is it? What's the matter?"

I could not speak but I pointed through the open door, and Mary went in. She was back again almost at once, her face very white, but she said almost steadily, "I'll phone for a doctor." She started down the stairs as Mrs. Markham, Barbara, and Dennis appeared from the third floor.

I gave them a brief, hysterical explanation and then suddenly felt violently sick. Barbara helped me up to my room, and we huddled together on my bed while I tried to get my stomach under control.

"I should be down there with Mama," Barbara said after a while.

I took a long breath and realized that I was feeling better. "Don't worry. Mary's there and Dennis. What could you do?"

"What could have *happened* to her?" Barbara said wonderingly. "Are you sure she was dead?"

"Listen," I said, feeling sick again. "Her face was all puffed and dark blue, and her eyes were sticking out like marbles."

Barbara shuddered and turned her face away. "I hate things like that," she muttered.

We stayed there for over an hour, smoking and listening to the sounds of subdued activity downstairs. Dennis came at last, knocking at the door and saying that we were wanted. He looked very serious and when we asked what was happening said soberly, "Doctor says she's been dead for some time—asphyxiation. He won't give a certificate and says it's a matter for the police."

Barbara stopped dead and moaned, "Police! Oh God! What's going to happen to the place? Everyone will leave—"

"Oh, I don't think so," Dennis said. "Probably a peculiar accident of some sort. The police will clear it up, and it will soon be forgotten."

But Barbara said, "I doubt it," and secretly I doubted it too.

Dennis took us to the dining room, and we passed a policeman who was ornamenting the front hall.

Everyone was in the dining room, including Evie and Kate, who were the only servants that Mrs. Markham employed. There were two strange men who appeared to be questioning Miss Giddens. Mrs. Markham sat by, trying to help, and as we came in one of the men said to her, "Madam, will you please allow the lady to answer the questions in her own way."

Mrs. Markham, who knew all about Miss Giddens' way, closed her lips in a firm line and waited for the three of them to get tangled up.

"Now, Miss Giddens," said the man, "how long was the body in your room?"

"It's *my* room," said Miss Giddens distinctly.

The man took a long breath, seemed to count up to ten, and said, "Yes, yes, certainly. It's your room. But I want you to answer a few questions."

Miss Giddens' attention had wandered. She was looking around at all the people in the room in a puzzled fashion.

"Miss Giddens!" the man said sharply.

She turned back to him, and he said quickly, "When did that woman come to visit you? The one who came to see you in your room and would not leave."

"She brought her sister with her," Miss Giddens observed and got up from her chair.

She was promptly reseated, gently but firmly.

"Who came with those two sisters?" he asked. "Who brought them to see you?"

Miss Giddens shook her head and asked of the room in general, "Is dinner ready?"

The man said, "Dinner is almost ready. Do you know where Miss Imogene Rostrum is?"

"No," said Miss Giddens vaguely, "I don't know."

"Did she say good-by to you when she left?"

Miss Giddens said "no" six times with gradually increasing annoyance.

"But wasn't it rude of her not to say good-by when she left ?"

"I'm not rude," said Miss Giddens, looking thoroughly offended. "I'm not rude at all. *You* are being very rude. But *I'm* not."

Grace spoke into a short silence. "Inspector, I don't think you're going to get anything out of her that way. If you let Mrs. Markham speak to her alone you can listen at the door and you'll get more sense from her.''

The man glared and said, "Will you kindly allow me to handle this in my own way, miss?"

The other man stirred, at that point, and said, "I'm Inspector Dodd. This is Sergeant Schmaltz." He added, "I think the suggestion has some merit, Schmaltz. You haven't got anything yet."

"At least I got that the sister was there and was taken out again," Schmaltz growled.

"She might have walked out."

Schmaltz said, "She might have—but what with that other portiere—"

"We'll have the house searched after we've finished here. I'll want everyone to wait in the living room."

"Drawing room," murmured Mrs. Markham bleakly.

"Don't quibble," said the inspector while Schmaltz hunched his shoulders and went on with the questioning. He had no trouble with the rest of us—it was merely a matter of what we had done and where we had been since yesterday and it was all very prosaic. Mrs. Markham, Camille, Kate, and Uncle Alvin had not left the house at all since the day before yesterday. Miss Giddens might or might not have taken one of her short walks—no one could clearly remember.

Mary and Grace had spent the evening at the movies, and Dennis had had a business appointment with a man named Davis who lived on Fifth Avenue, down Washington Square way. I was a little surprised when this piece of information came out and found myself wondering what sort of business, other than mine, could be occupying Dennis in New York.

Neville had spent the evening playing solitaire in the drawing room and had retired at ten o'clock and gone straight to bed.

Evie had been out for two nights in succession. The first night had taken her to a dance palace and the second to a movie.

"She goes runnin' out all the time," Kate volunteered. Schmaltz snapped, "So what? She's a young girl, ain't she?" and received a nice smile from Evie.

Sounds of sudden activity came from the hall, and Inspector Dodd stood up. "If you will all stay until we have a look at the living room. . ."

Mrs. Markham's lips moved, but she didn't actually say it.

"I shall want you to wait in the living room after we have finished there," said Inspector Dodd and took himself off, followed closely by Schmaltz.

Dennis wandered to the door after them and stood peering into the corridor that led to the front hall. "It's the ambulance, I think," he said after a moment. "They have a stretcher."

He returned to his chair, and I got up restlessly and looked out myself. The front hall seemed to be filled with men. "Who on earth can they be?" I asked over my shoulder.

Dennis murmured, "Photographers, fingerprint experts, medical examiner."

I went back to my chair and wondered why I was still being shaken by occasional spasms of trembling.

"What could have happened?" Mrs. Markham moaned, wringing her hands.

"She must have committed suicide," Camille said harshly. "It was gas, wasn't it?"

Neville said, "Yes. She had been dead from twenty to twenty-five hours."

"How do you know?" Mary asked wearily.

"I heard them say so."

There was a short silence, and then I said fearfully, "Where is the other portiere?"

"That's what they're going to search for," Grace said. "I think they figure that when they find that they'll find Miss Imogene."

I saw Barbara shiver and I began to tremble again.

Mrs. Markham said suddenly, "Barbara. You told me that they stared at you in a peculiar way yesterday, just before they disappeared."

"They did," Barbara said slowly. "They stared at me as though they saw something very odd."

I confirmed this. "We both thought it was very queer. They'd known Barbara for years and yet they stared at her as though they'd never seen her before."

"I don't see why they should commit suicide just because Barbara's slip was showing or she had a spot on her nose," Camille said, nervously swinging a plump leg back and forth.

"I don't see how it could possibly be suicide," Dennis said sharply. "They could hardly have wrapped themselves in those portieres and moved into Miss Giddens' room after they were dead."

"Maybe they died in there," Camille said sulkily.

"She must still have wrapped herself in the portiere first," Dennis pointed out, "which doesn't make sense. Add to that the fact that Miss Giddens slept in her room on the same night that Miss Opal committed suicide in there and was not affected "

"All right, all right," Camille interrupted, still sulky. "You don't have to be sarcastic."

"Besides," said Neville, "I heard the medical examiner say that Miss Opal had been struck on the head."

Mary twisted her hands together and muttered, "My God! Then it's murder, all right. And Miss Imogene, lying around somewhere in that black portiere—murdered too."

We were silent after that, for a long time. I stared dully at the oak sideboard that had always fascinated me. It was elaborately carved and had a huge mirror and a sort of roof at the top. My eyes wandered to the roof now—and were held there, bulging.

The missing black portiere lay there, neatly folded.

CHAPTER EIGHT

I STARTED TO MY FEET and cried out, "Look! There's the other portiere—and Miss Imogene isn't—isn't wrapped in it!"

They all stood up and looked—and somehow, a weight seemed to be lifted from us because that portiere so obviously did not conceal the body of Miss Imogene.

Neville walked to the door of the drawing room after a while and called to Schmaltz in a peremptory sort of way. I don't know whether he actually called him "my man," but that was the sort of voice. Schmaltz was irritable, but he followed Neville to the dining room and barked, "Well, what is it?"

"It's the other portiere," Camille said shrilly, and Schmaltz reached up and pulled it down. As he unfolded it a speck of white fell out and drifted to the floor. I stooped and picked it up, and Schmaltz asked, "What was that?"

"I don't know." I opened my hand and exposed what appeared to be a small triangular piece of paper. Schmaltz glanced at it, said, "Yup," and appeared to lose interest. I closed my hand again, and Schmaltz refolded the portiere.

"All right," he said. "Just stick around here until I finish the living room." He departed, and we gloomily resumed our chairs.

After a while Barbara jabbed my arm and whispered, "Remember that hole somebody dug in the tulip bed? Maybe Miss Imogene is in it."

I started to shiver and said through my banging teeth, "I—I don't think so. I think she'd—be wrapped in that portiere if she were."

"Do you think it was meant to be a grave?"

I nodded. "I think they were both going to be buried there, wrapped in the portiere, only Miss Giddens spoiled things by fussing about Miss Opal having been left in her room." I closed my eyes for a moment and added, "What a gruesome thing to do. I suppose they thought Miss Giddens was too fuzzy to notice anything."

Camille asked sharply, "What are you girls talking about?"

We explained, and by the time we had finished somebody noticed that Uncle Alvin was missing. No one could account for him, and we were still wondering about him when it was discovered that Miss Giddens had disappeared too.

We sat in subdued silence until Schmaltz returned. He was accompanied by Miss Giddens, who peered at us in a puzzled fashion through his crooked elbow. He said, "All right—will you come into the living room now, please. And will you *please* keep this lady with you."

Miss Giddens shied away from the thumb that he jerked at her and preceded us into the drawing room with her nose in the air. We all sat down except Kate and Evie, who stood uneasily in the background.

After we were all settled we discovered that Uncle Alvin was with us once more, and Grace asked, "Where were you?"

He blinked and mumbled, "What?"

"Where did you go?" she asked impatiently. "Before. When we were in the dining room."

"Oh. I just went upstairs for a handkerchief." As though to prove it he pulled a handkerchief out of his pocket and blew his nose.

Mary stood up abruptly and began to pace the room. "I'm getting tired of all this," she said nervously.

From her place against the wall, in the shadows, Kate exploded into speech. "*You're* getting tired! What about us common folks? I suppose we gotta stand because our backsides ain't good enough for the fancy chairs!"

"That will do, Kate," said Mrs. Markham sharply. "Sit down at once. You, too, Evie."

Kate perched herself grimly on the edge of a chair while Evie dropped onto a couch and lounged back comfortably.

I got up restlessly and peered through the sliding doors into the dining room, where they were just finishing what appeared to be a sketchy search. As I looked they went on into the kitchen.

"What are they searching for, anyway?" I asked, turning back.

"Miss Imogene, of course," said Mary. "She's bound to be lying around somewhere. Those two always did everything together."

Grace cried, "Mary!" in a shocked voice, and after that we were silent until Inspector Dodd and Schmaltz came to us and said that we might go to bed.

Mrs. Markham stood up and asked briskly, but with a proper gravity, "Did you find Miss Imogene?"

Inspector Dodd said courteously, "No, but I think we should locate her in a matter of hours. I shall want to question each of you separately, early in the morning. Right now, I want you each to go to your own room as we have still a lot of detail work to see to."

Barbara and I spoke up more or less together and advised him to look in the back yard. I think I had expected him to rush straight out there, but instead of that, he gave us an odd look and asked us what we knew about the hole that had been dug. We explained carefully, but when we had finished it seemed to me that Inspector Dodd looked highly suspicious and that Schmaltz looked suspicious along with him.

I caught at Barbara's hand, and we almost ran up the stairs with an uneasy feeling that Dodd and Schmaltz were close behind with the handcuffs.

When we reached the third floor Mrs. Markham ordered Barbara straight to bed and gave me a look that plainly encouraged me to do likewise.

To relieve her mind, we assured her that we would go straight to sleep and after she had disappeared into her room we both went into mine and arranged ourselves comfortably on the bed.

"Too bad to deceive her," Barbara said, "but it's just too much to ask me to go to sleep now."

We lighted cigarettes and watched the smoke drift up past the neat, printed sign that said smoking was prohibited in this bedroom by order of the fire department.

Barbara glanced at the sign and scowled. "That's the government for you. We pay taxes to support a fire department, and the lazy punks don't want to climb three stories to put a fire out."

I discovered that I was still clutching the white fragment that had fallen from the portiere and I opened my fingers and looked at it idly.

After a moment I said with sudden concentration, "Look, Barbara. This isn't paper—it's a bit of organdy."

Barbara turned her head, studied the scrap, and eventually yawned, "So what?"

"Well—but this dropped from the portiere when Schmaltz shook it out."

She looked again, her forehead wrinkling in a faint frown.

"You know those bits of organdy collars or edging they always wore on their dresses? The Rostrums, I mean."

She nodded and said slowly, "Miss Imogene was wearing that green print—and the collar was edged with organdy. And I guess that means she was wrapped in that portiere, just as her sister was wrapped in the other one."

"We ought to go and tell Schmaltz."

"Well, yes—except they've searched the whole house already and haven't found her."

"But she *must* be around somewhere," I said hysterically. "We ought to look for her."

"Why not?" Barbara said suddenly. "I know this house much better than the police do, every nook and cranny of it. Come on—if she's in the house at all we'll find her."

Any activity was better than just sitting there, so I followed her out into the hall, and we leaned over the banister and listened for a few minutes. Everything seemed to be quiet, and we presently crept cautiously down the stairs. The hall on the second floor was empty and still, and we went on down to the first floor. The dim night light still burned in the front hall, but the rest of the place was in darkness.

Barbara glanced around and then whispered, "My guess is that she has already been dumped into that hole in the yard."

I shook my head. "Dodd and Schmaltz seemed to know all about that hole, and anyway, if she'd been put in there I think she would have been left in the portiere."

"I think we ought to look there first, just the same."

I shrugged, and we started out toward the pantry. The swinging door leading to the kitchen was closed, but we could see a line of light along the bottom, and it was quite clear that someone was eating in there. We could hear the whole process.

"They've left a man behind," I whispered into Barbara's ear.

We backed away quietly and returned to the front of the house. "I suppose it was a policeman," Barbara said doubtfully.

"The dumbest burglar would have instinct enough to keep away from here tonight."

We took a couple of warm coats from the hall closet—Barbara's belonged to her mother and mine to Camille—and let ourselves out the front door. We set the lock so that we could get back in again and made our way around to the back, keeping close against the side of the house.

The first thing we saw was a white patch on the ground directly under Miss Giddens' window, that turned out to be her shawl. Barbara bunched it under her arm, and we continued on to the tulip bed.

The hole was still there, but it seemed a bit larger than it had been the night before. We soon satisfied ourselves that Miss Imogene was not there, but we were now thoroughly convinced that the tulip bed had been intended as a grave for both sisters.

Someone opened a window in the house above us, and we hastily crouched down, but it was only Miss Giddens. She stuck her head out for a moment and then drew it in and closed the window.

"Uncle Alvin is still awake too," Barbara whispered, indicating the lighted widow on the fourth floor. "Poor dear—I suppose he's all upset. He and the Rostrums were always good friends'"

"You can tell me the family history when we get inside," I said impatiently. "I'm freezing."

We made our way around the house and up the steps but as we started to push the door open we saw the policeman, probably well fed by this time and slowly pacing up and down. He had his back to us, and just before he turned around we quietly closed the door and stood on tile stoop outside, looking at each other.

"What do we do now?" I asked, hugging Camille's too voluminous coat around me and shivering until my teeth rattled.

Barbara glanced along the narrow iron balcony that edged the bay windows of the drawing room. "Come on," she said, pushing me toward it. "One of the windows may be open."

We scrambled onto the balcony as best we could in the darkness. The night seemed to have become unusually black, and I wondered vaguely if it were getting ready to dawn.

There was a small, wrought-iron loveseat at the end of the balcony, and as Barbara started fumbling with the windows I groped my way along and sat down.

It took me a moment to realize that someone was sitting beside me—and as horror flooded darkly through me my hand touched a thin silk sleeve that clothed a marble-cold arm.

CHAPTER NINE

WHEN I COULD SPEAK AT ALL I heard my voice come out in a hollow whisper. "Oh, Barbara! Quick! What is it?"

She was busy at one of the windows and she muttered in a preoccupied voice, "What's the matter?"

I managed to get out of the seat although I was shaking so that I could hardly stand. I made my way through the darkness until, with a quick little breath of relief, I bumped into Barbara. She said again, with a touch of irritation, "What's the matter?"

I swallowed a scream that had been pressing at the back of my throat and chattered, "She's there. Sitting over there on that seat—and she's dead."

Barbara quavered, "Oh God! What do you mean? How do you know?"

"She's cold—she's deathly cold. We'll have to get someone—that policeman."

We went straight in the front door that time, and I think we gave the policeman more of a start than he would have cared to admit. But as soon as we had told our excited, hysterical story he went into action without any delay. We led him out to the balcony, and he produced a flashlight and played it over the loveseat. The circle of light came to rest at last, directly upon Miss Imogene's purple, bloated face—and I went straight to the railing, leaned my head over, and lost the day's nourishment. When I was able to turn around the light had dropped from the face and was playing over the body, and I was surprised at how natural it looked.

The policeman ordered us inside at that point and told us to wait in the hall. We went in and huddled together on the stairs. Barbara was crying quietly. "I've known them for so long," she whispered, mopping at her eyes. "It's so beastly, to hurt two old ladies who never harmed anyone."

I wanted to cry, too, but I gritted my teeth and said, "There's no sense to it. I don't suppose they had any money?"

"Nothing they could leave to anyone," Barbara replied, shaking her head. "Their money had been put into insurance annuities—and of course the income stops when they die. And I'm sure their personal possessions have no value."

We sat there until Inspector Dodd and Schmaltz arrived with a full retinue. I watched the activity through a daze of shock and fatigue, and after a while Barbara and I were put through a grueling questionnaire which left us with only strength enough to creep up to the third floor when we were finally released.

It was growing light by this time, but the upstairs halls were still blank and quiet.

"How *could* they sleep through all that milling around down there?" I said wonderingly.

"I bet every one of 'em woke up," Barbara whispered. "They probably listened at their doors—but you can't blame them for wanting to avoid a tangle with dear old Schmaltz."

I think the fact that it was daylight helped me to relax a little, and as soon as I got into bed I fell at once into an exhausted sleep. But at nine o'clock I opened my eyes and was wide awake. I knew that I could not get off again, so I dressed and went on downstairs. The front hall was ornamented by some strange men, but I did not see either Schmaltz or Inspector Dodd. They ignored me, so I went on through to the dining room.

Evie followed routine by informing me that breakfast was really over but that she'd see what she could do for me. She promptly produced my usual breakfast and then hung over me, conversing sociably while I tried to eat it. She had noticed a loafer, she said, loitering around the place for some weeks past. I showed little interest in the loafer, so she offered the tidbit that Camille had owed the Rostrums some money.

"That isn't worth the breath you wasted on it," I said, pouring coffee. "Camille owes money to all of us—even you, I bet."

Evie adjusted her apron and said sulkily, "Well, yes, she does, and I wish she'd pay me back. She owes me a dollar fifty."

"What does she owe Kate?" I asked.

Evie hooted as loudly as she dared. "If anybody ever got a nickel offa that one I'd like to be introduced."

"What are the cops doing this morning?" I asked.

She shrugged. "Search me. They followed me and Kate around the kitchen, back there a while, astin' us anything they could think of like what dentist do we go to and when did we stop believin' in Santa Claus."

She sniffed, and I asked, "How long have you and Kate been here?"

"I've worked here the last five years," said Evie, "and I mean *worked*."

I said, "Oh, cheese it. Mrs. Markham and Barbara do most of the work around here. I've seen them."

"Don't you kid yourself," Evie said earnestly. "They do the sissy stuff like putting flowers around and fluffing up pillows. I do all the hard work."

"All right—but how long has Kate worked here?"

"I dunno—ten years, maybe. But listen, if you're gonna ast questions like that Schmaltz I'm goin' back to the kitchen."

"Oh no, you're not," I said. "You know darned well you're safe here with me. If you go back to the kitchen you'll be put back to hard labor."

She wandered off around the room, straightened one or two of the tables, and brushed off some imaginary crumbs. "You don't think I'm loafing here, do you?" she asked, aggrieved. "I'm merely doing my dooty. One of Mrs. Markham's strick rules is always be polite to the guests. So if you talk I gotta listen."

"I'd like to talk," I said, "if I could get a word in edgewise. How do the cops get you into a listening mood?"

She said, "Say, listen—" And at that moment Mrs. Markham appeared at the door. Evie disappeared between my taking a mouthful of coffee and getting it past my tonsils.

Mrs. Markham glanced at the pantry door, which was still quivering, and frowned absently. After a moment's hesitation she came and sat down at the table with me.

"This is a bad business," she said heavily. "I'm afraid the place will be ruined. Nobody will want to stay."

"I think it will work out all right," I said, more from a desire to comfort her than from any conviction. "It's surprising how quickly things blow over, especially in New York."

She shook her head unhappily. "You know, I've known the Rostrums since they were girls—they used to live across the street. But I can't imagine anyone wanting to do them harm, they were so inoffensive."

I nodded and asked, "Didn't they have any relatives?"

"There are some cousins in Connecticut, but they're not coming down. I had a telegram from them this morning, asking me to take charge of everything."

"Aren't there any friends?"

"Outside of the hotel, there was one woman who came to see them about once in three months, but I don't know of anyone else."

"Have the police discovered anything yet?" I asked.

"Not that I know of, but I don't suppose they'd confide in me, in any case. They're still trying to get some sense out of Miss Giddens about what actually happened in her room."

"Waste of the taxpayers' money," I said. "There isn't any sense in Miss Giddens."

"I'm afraid they'll find it quite hopeless," she agreed.

"I think you're the only one who could get anywhere with Miss Giddens," I suggested after a moment's thought. "Let's get her in here and see what you can do."

"I'm very willing to do what I can," she said with a little sigh. "The sooner the thing is cleared up, the better it will be for me."

"How long has Miss Giddens been here?" I asked.

"About seven years, I think."

Evie appeared from the kitchen and swished her way to the front hall. Mrs. Markham glanced after her, and the worry in her eyes sparkled into annoyance. "She's inclined to be impertinent, I'm afraid. You must let me know if ever she is rude to you."

"Oh yes, certainly," I lied and knew quite well that I'd never tell on Evie.

She appeared behind us at that moment and said, "Gentleman to see you, miss."

I raised my head and stared at the heavy-set man who loomed behind her. "That's not a gentleman, Evie," I said. "That's Papa."

CHAPTER TEN

"IF I'M NOT A GENTLEMAN," said Papa crossly, "I've wasted a lot of time helping women into cars, allowing them to precede me through doors, and snatching my blasted hat off in elevators to show that I have respect for womankind."

"All right—you can keep your shirt on, even if you have to take off your hat," I said and kissed him. "It's good to see you, even if I'm mad at you."

"Never mind the mush," said Papa. "Pack your traps, and we'll leave at once."

I backed away. "What are you talking about? What makes you think the police would allow me to leave?"

He stared at me for a moment and then removed his overcoat and sat down. "So you're in a real jam. Okay, let's have it. All I know is that the police phoned me and asked me if you were my daughter, so I drove down at once."

Mrs. Markham, all graciousness, dispatched Evie to get him some breakfast and then left us alone while I told him the whole story.

Toward the end of my recital he exploded. "Dammit, girl, can't you keep out of trouble? I can't leave you swilling around in a mess like this, and my affairs are very pressing right now."

"They're always pressing," I said. "Maybe they'll ease up a bit if you leave them alone for a while. Anyway, if you're going to stay, stay, but don't crab about it. I can introduce you to a lovely girl, just about your age. Name's Miss Giddens."

"Be quiet," said Papa. "You know I'm through with women for good and all."

"Since when?" I asked. "Yesterday?"

He plowed his way through a whopping big breakfast and then proceeded to make himself as much a pest to Dodd and Schmaltz as Miss Giddens was. They managed to convince him at last that it would be pleasanter all around if I stayed at Mrs. Markham's for a while.

"Naturally," Papa told me later, "they couldn't really hold you, but I always think it looks better to work with the police, rather than against them."

That was at eleven o'clock, and at five minutes past Camille caught sight of him, and I saw no more of him until lunch time.

Meanwhile Barbara and I had a talk with Mrs. Markham at her own request. She asked us to come into her room, and it was the first time I had been there. It was large and airy and had twin beds because Barbara had to bunk in there on the rare occasions when the house was full. It was very neat and rather bare, and the only ornaments were a few old photographs on the bureau.

We sat down, and Mrs. Markham said, "I wanted to suggest something to you girls because you're young, and young eyes often notice things that older people might miss." She drew a quick sigh and went on, "I've worked this house up to a paying proposition but I'm afraid it is doomed unless our trouble is cleared up very quickly, so that people may have a chance to forget.

"Now I don't want you children to do any such dangerous investigating as you did last night, but you can keep your eyes open and you may notice something. Remember, you know all these people. You would be working from the inside while the police must work from the outside. And if you find anything, girls, you must tell the police at once. Don't attempt to keep anything to yourselves."

Barbara said, "Oh sure, Mama, we'll do our best for you. We'll have it all solved in no time."

She seemed quite enthusiastic, and Mrs. Markham smiled a trifle wearily. "I don't mean that exactly, dear. I doubt if you could solve a thing like this. I meant that you might be able to help the police to solve it. I want you to tell them things—things you might notice that they would not because you know the people here and can tell more quickly when something is not as it should be. I believe you could be a real help to the police in that way.

"And now I want you to find Miss Giddens and bring her to me. We might be able to get something intelligent from her."

Barbara and I went off in search of the old lady, and on our way downstairs I said, "Schmaltz was a dope not to let your mother help with Miss Giddens."

Barbara nodded. "We'll get it out of her now, though, if it's to be got."

We finally ran Miss Giddens to earth in the kitchen, where she was perched comfortably on Kate's chair. There were two straight chairs in the kitchen, and Kate had appropriated to herself the one that had arms.

She was talking to herself in an aggrieved mumble, and as soon as she caught sight of us the mumble became intelligent. "I'll go stark crazy if someone don't keep that old pest outa my kitchen. I got to have eyes in the back of my head, or she's eatin' everything in sight. I can put a bib on her and feed her, or I can feed the rest of the house, but it ain't to be expected that I can do both."

Miss Giddens rarely heard anything that was said about her, but apparently this penetrated, and she raised her head and stared at Kate with sharp annoyance. "You will stick to your pots and kettles, Cook, and save your impertinence for when it's wanted," she said haughtily.

Kate's mouth dropped open for a moment. "Well, will you listen to that!" she yelled, recovering. "What's got into her?"

Barbara giggled and said, "Miss Giddens, Mother would like to see you."

Miss Giddens gave us the same attention she might have bestowed on the kitchen sink and wandered off. We followed her through the dining room and into the drawing room, where we came abreast of her, one on each side, and tried to steer her toward the hall. She took a look out of the front window first, and then we were able to edge her into the hall and up the stairs. On the second floor, however, she suddenly darted away from us, slipped into her room and shut the door in our faces.

"Damn it!" said Barbara.

A shocked voice behind us said, "Please don't use expressions like that, my dear. You're so young."

We turned to find Uncle Alvin blinking anxiously at us, and I saw Barbara's face soften. She knew that he was fond of her and she said cheerfully, "All right, I'll keep it clean. But only for you, remember."

He smiled happily. "You know, the police won't let me fix the tulip bed, and I'm afraid the bulbs are going to be spoiled."

"Who dug them up?" I asked. "Was it you?"

"I? No, no! I had put them in, all snug, just a short time ago, and then someone goes and digs them up. I think it was done deliberately—spite, you know."

Barbara said, "Now listen, Uncle Alvin, why would anyone want to get even with you? You've never done anything to anyone."

"Oh, I don't know," he said vaguely. "People are funny sometimes. There's Camille—been mad at me for a couple of weeks. I wouldn't take her to the movies a while back, and she can't get over it."

"Oh, Camille will come round," Barbara assured him. "Don't pay any attention to her."

"But do you think she could have dug up my tulips?"

Barbara shook her head. "It would be good exercise for her hips, but she's too lazy for anything like that."

"I suppose you're right." He gave a short sigh and added, "But she did say she'd get even with me sometime."

He went off, and Barbara looked after him with a little frown "I wish Camille would leave him alone, but she's still man-crazy even at her age."

I said, "Come on, let's go in and get Miss Giddens. Your mother is waiting."

"Okay." She turned to Miss Giddens' door, opened it, and walked straight in, while I followed with a certain amount of diffidence.

Miss Giddens was sitting in her rocking chair, and she continued to sway slowly as she raised her head and blinked her small black eyes at us. Apparently we did not interest her, for she shifted her gaze to the window and started to chew the cud, which was more or less usual when she was not actually eating.

"Mother wants to see you," Barbara said brightly.

Miss Giddens stopped rocking, stared at Barbara, and slowly shook her head.

"Don't you want to see Mother?"

Miss Giddens shook her head more vigorously and put the chair into motion again, as though the matter were closed.

Barbara said, "All right, but she has some candy she wants to give you."

The chair slowed to a stop, and Miss Giddens chewed on for a space and then hoisted herself to her feet.

We walked her up to Mrs. Markham's room without any trouble and found Mrs. Markham taking a nap, which I knew to be unusual at that time in the morning. However, she woke up, briskly put herself to rights, and led Miss Giddens to a chair.

"Where's the candy, Mother?" Barbara asked significantly.

Mrs. Markham raised her eyebrows, caught on, and shrugged. "I'm afraid I haven't any."

Miss Giddens got up and started for the door.

"Wait a minute," I cried. "I have some in my room. I'll get it."

I brought a full box of chocolates, and we placed it in Miss Giddens' lap. She went straight to work on it, and by the time we had finished with her, there were only a few pieces left in the bottom.

The interview lasted for about half an hour, and I admired the way Mrs. Markham handled it. She plowed through a lot of preliminaries first and then asked, "When did the two ladies—Miss Opal and Miss Imogene come to visit you?"

"Yes," said Miss Giddens, nodding her head. "Yes, they came to visit. 'Twas very kind of them."

"Did they visit you today?"

"Oh no—not today. I don't think it was today."

"Did they visit you yesterday?" Mrs. Markham asked gently.

Miss Giddens thought it over while she took another chocolate. Finally, she nodded and said, "Yes. Yes, they came to visit yesterday."

I knew that they had both been dead yesterday and I shuddered.

But Mrs. Markham went on quietly, "Did they come yesterday morning or yesterday afternoon?"

"Yes," said Miss Giddens amiably.

"Was it in the morning?" Mrs. Markham persisted.

"Yes."

"It was not in the afternoon, then?"

"No," said Miss Giddens and appeared to lose interest in everything but the candy.

"Who else came with Miss Opal and Miss Imogene?" Mrs. Markham asked slowly and clearly.

Miss Giddens looked up. "Yes," she said. "That man."

CHAPTER ELEVEN

BARBARA AND I NEARLY STOPPED breathing while Mrs. Markham went on quietly, "Yes, the man who came to visit you with Miss Opal and Miss Imogene—he was their friend—a friend of Miss Opal and Miss Imogene."

Miss Giddens half nodded and took another chocolate.

Mrs. Markham moved closer and tried to hold the old lady's attention by staring into her face. "Who was this man—this friend of Miss Opal's and Miss Imogene's? Did you know him?"

"Yes, I know him," said Miss Giddens impatiently. "An old friend of mine. Quite an old friend."

"Is he one of the men who lives here with us?"

Miss Giddens helped herself to another chocolate.

"Was it Alvin who visited you with Miss Opal and Miss Imogene?" No answer.

"Was it Neville who came to visit you?"

Miss Giddens, chewing vigorously, stuck her foot out and studied her shoe.

Mrs. Markham made another effort. "The man who came to visit you with Miss Opal and Miss Imogene—did he have to carry them in? Were they sick, so that he had to carry them?"

Miss Giddens looked up and nodded. "Yes, they were sick—very sick. He carried them in and put them on my floor, and all day they could not speak. They were very ill, you know. I gave them a peppermint, but they did not want it. Then they went home, and I went down to dinner—and then there was that woman, and she stayed and stayed. I did not like her—I didn't like her face."

We were all breathing on tiptoe by that time. Mrs. Markham shifted very slightly in her chair and went on, "When did she come? The woman who stayed in your room—the woman you didn't like."

"All night," said Miss Giddens. "She was there all night, and I did not like her face. I told them I didn't like it. They shouldn't make so free with my room. It's mine, isn't it?"

"Of course it's your room," Mrs. Markham said soothingly.

Miss Giddens had one of her lucid flashes and rose to her feet. "Then I think I'll go to it. I've had a very pleasant time—very kind of you." She padded out of the room with my candy box tucked under her arm.

Mrs. Markham sighed and relaxed into her chair. "Well, that was something. But I'll get after her again. I think she has more to tell if I can only get it out of her."

"I wonder if there's anything to the man she mentioned," Barbara said thoughtfully. "There's only Uncle Alvin and Neville in the house."

"There's Dennis," I said, sniffing. "Papa, too, now."

"Well, but your father wasn't here, Diana," Mrs. Markham said, "so we must count him out. Of course, we'll have to consider Mr. Livingstone—" She stopped suddenly, with a little breath of exasperation. "It's all so absurd! What reason could any of those men have, to have harmed two old ladies? Why would anyone do such a thing? But there must be a reason, and perhaps we can discover something, since our opportunities are better than those of the police.

"You'd better run along now, girls—and for heaven's sake, don't get into any trouble. Keep your eyes open but don't do anything. Come and ask me first."

"Shouldn't we tell the police about what we got out of Miss Giddens?" Barbara asked.

"No, dear, I think not. It's too vague and inconclusive. Tomorrow will be time enough, in any case, and in the meantime perhaps we can pick up something more."

Barbara and I went off to the bathroom to wash up for lunch. It was at the back of the house, and the window overlooked the yard, so that we could see the black hole that still yawned in the tulip bed.

Barbara frowned and said, "I wish they'd fill in that grave. It makes me sick at my stomach every time I see it."

I felt sick myself but I said hastily, "Come on, let's go down and see Papa—and then you can get a laugh."

But it appeared that she had a few hurried duties to perform before lunch, so I went on down alone.

Papa was in the drawing room, boring Camille to the point of tears. He was giving her his life's history and had got to the technical side of pea canning. I stood in the empty archway for a while and listened.

Camille was making occasional efforts to steer him away to something more lively, but each time he merely raised his voice, drowned her out, and continued steadily with the canning business.

I went in and broke it up. "You can have someone type it, Papa," I said cheerfully. "Have about one hundred and fifty copies made, and then you can hand them out and save time and eardrums."

"I'll tell my ruddy life history whenever I please," he said rudely. "I'm old, ugly, and rich enough to do what I like, and anyway, I've never found anyone but you who wasn't interested."

But Camille had been given her chance, and she took it promptly. "My dear," she said to me, "don't go out, whatever you do. There are reporters of all descriptions lying in wait. I had a perfectly terrible time. Six or eight of them surrounded me, and I simply had to tell them everything, until that crude fellow, Schmaltz, came and rescued me."

Papa nodded. "We're marooned. You stick inside and play with your paper dolls, Di. I don't want those fellows to know I'm here."

I said, "Try to be a little bright, Papa. Of course they know you're here. The movements of Quincy Prescott, the well-known canner, would always be watched and reported."

He made no reply, and I saw that he was staring over my shoulder with an expression of surprise and anger. I turned to find Dennis behind me, just as Papa said in a low, quivering voice, "You damned worm!"

"Nice to see you too," Dennis said, apparently quite unperturbed.

"It's just like you fellows who pretend to be so noble," Papa hissed. "Couldn't stay away from the place, could you? You wouldn't come here when I asked you to, but you sneak around behind my back. And don't think I don't know why, either. You didn't know I had a daughter before, did you? But when I tell you I have one you first act noble and crawl around when I'm not looking and try to marry her so you'll be fixed for life—"

"Papa, wait," I said as he paused for breath. "Let me get this straight. You approached Mr. Livingstone on the matter of coming here and making love to me, so that I could be lured home?"

"Certainly,'' he replied without any vestige of shame. "But I made it quite clear that he was only to pretend—he was not to be really serious, and as soon as he got you home he was to quit."

"I see," I said grimly. "Not only did you want to get me back to the sticks, but once there you wanted to turn me into a brokenhearted old maid."

Dennis laughed, and Papa said, "Shut up, you! Now, listen, honey," he added, turning to me, "it was only that I didn't want you to marry him. I wanted somebody better for you. There are plenty of men around—you can practically have your pick. But this skunk refused to do what I asked. We got into a row, so I fired him."

"Oh no, you didn't," Dennis interrupted coldly. "I resigned."

"But, Papa," I said uncomfortably. "You can't turn people out of their jobs because they refuse you personal favors."

He turned about face and said hotly, "I didn't—he resigned on his own hook. And now I see why. He rushed straight up here to try and marry you behind my back."

I began to feel distinctly embarrassed. A hasty glance around showed me that Uncle Alvin and Neville had come upon the scene and were listening with their ears flapping.

But Papa, with no sense of shame at all, was still bellowing, "Have you the infernal gall to deny that you practically broke a leg getting down here so that you could grab my daughter for yourself?"

"I deny it most emphatically," said Dennis, still cold, and adding a little hauteur. "I have no interest in your snubnosed daughter, Prescott. I came here because my godmother, Miss Opal Rostrum, wrote me that something was frightening her."

CHAPTER TWELVE

CAMILLE GAVE A HIGH nervous laugh while the rest of us stared in silence.

Papa spoke at last and sounded rather like Schmaltz. "She was one of those who was murdered, wasn't she?"

Dennis said, "Yes."

"Well, what was scaring her?" I asked quickly, and overlooking the fact that he had called me snubnosed.

"I think she was not quite sure," Dennis replied. "In any case, what information I have has been given to the police."

"But listen," Camille put in curiously. "You were introduced to the Rostrums and you all acted like strangers to each other."

"That was Miss Opal's idea," Dennis explained. "I suppose she thought if I came as a stranger I should have a better chance to do a little investigating and perhaps clear up what was bothering her. As a matter of fact, I suggested that they move to another place, but Miss Opal would not hear of it. She said that this was their home."

"Coincidence," said Papa, raising his eyebrows, "has a very long arm at times."

The luncheon gong rang just then, and we all stirred. Uncle Alvin disappeared into the dining room at once, and Neville pulled out his old-fashioned gold watch and frowned at it. Camille linked arms with Papa and coyly asked him to escort her into the dining room. Papa escorted her perforce, and the next thing, I found Dennis beside me with his arm crooked.

"May I escort you into the dining room?" he asked.

I said, "No. You've humiliated me all over the lot, and the less I see of you, the better."

He looked somewhat offended and said, "As you wish." Although what he had to be offended about, when he had just finished calling me snubnosed, I don't know.

In the dining room I found that I had been moved to a small table with Papa. I sat down and asked innocently, "Wouldn't you rather sit with your girlfriend, Camille? It would be all right because I could move back with Barbara."

It didn't work. Papa narrowed his eyes and said out of the corner of his mouth, "You stay where you are. I'll see plenty of that turkey and I'm entitled to an intermission when I can get it."

He was about two thirds through his meal when Schmaltz appeared and took him away for questioning. He went quietly—partly, I believe, because he thought that now he would have an interested audience for the story of his life.

Dennis left the dining room shortly after that and drifted to a stop at my table. "My apologies, Miss Prescott," he said in a low voice, "for having called you snubnosed. It was unkind."

I said, "Not at all—it was downright silly. Because I'm not."

He gave a murmur that might or might not have been assent and moved off.

Mrs. Markham and Barbara had just come in, and since I had finished I moved over to their table.

"Heard the latest?" I asked.

They showed a flattering interest, so I told them all about Miss Opal and Dennis. "Dennis and I are only speaking politely at the moment," I added, "so I thought maybe Barbara could dig out of him what it was Miss Opal was frightened about."

"Sure," said Barbara. "I like that assignment."

Mrs. Markham sighed, and two little creases appeared between her eyebrows. "I suppose you might, dear. But don't"—she hesitated, and the frown deepened—"don't cheapen yourself."

"Why, Mama!" Barbara said and laughed. "Now what in the world could you mean?"

"Now, Barbara! You know very well what I mean," Mrs. Markham said with a touch of severity.

I left them then because I was dying for some sleep and had made up my mind to take a long nap. In the front hall Papa waylaid me and shook his head at me with a look of gloom. "I suppose you realize that this is a bad business? It beats me why girls of your age are always straining at the bit to rush off and get into trouble."

"I didn't get into trouble," I said crossly. "Can I help it if people kill other people while I'm living in the house?"

"You should stay home where you belong," he snapped. "Do you know the police are highly suspicious of you? They wanted to know all about you."

I sat down on the stairs because I was suddenly so scared that my knees wobbled. But I continued to look defiantly at Papa. "They want to know all about everybody, naturally. And who can tell them better about me than you? Besides, I—found them."

"That's just it!" he said, rumpling his hair. "I wish you wouldn't be such a damned snoop. You find one of them and then you find the other—and it looks phony. I told them you always found your Christmas presents by the twentieth of December, no matter where I hid them, but I don't think it went over. Your finding the second one was just plain damn foolishness, what with the police already having searched for her."

"And I can't help it if I'm brighter than the police, either," I said, still cross. "Why don't you go and take a nap in your luxury suite—while I do likewise in my third-floor rear?"

I started up the stairs, and he called after me, "Don't think you can work any sympathy out of me over that rathole of a bedroom. After all, you have a rich father, and I haven't. I have to make my own way."

I ignored him and went on up to the third floor. I stretched out on my bed and then got up again to lock the door. Settled down once more, I was rather dismayed to find that I could not sleep even though I was so desperately tired. Miss Opal's blue distorted face kept swimming into my consciousness, and I could not get her out of my mind. The police had said asphyxiation—gas. But where was there any gas? They had disappeared right after dinner—right in the middle of their dinners, really. Perhaps they had been gassed in the kitchen then. But they would have had to be taken there after everyone was in bed. And then they'd have had to be carried up to Miss Giddens' room. That would require a man, and a strong one. I did not think that Uncle Alvin could have managed it and I was very doubtful about Neville too. Dennis could do it, of course, but why would he want to? They hadn't left any money, unless there was some we didn't know about.

I turned my pillow over and decided to put it all out of my mind and at the same time I was busily thinking that there was no garage on the premises, and so it must have been the kitchen. But what an odd way of killing people.

I found myself staring at the electric-light fixture and suddenly I concentrated on it. It was a plain metal suspension from the center of the ceiling and must have been installed after the house was built. A small arm depended down and out at the bottom and ended in the fancy, scalloped glass shade that covered the bulb. Slightly higher, another arm curved upward in the opposite direction.

I sat up and stared. But of course all the rooms had gas jets. It was something that I had often seen and yet never really noticed.

I lay down again and considered it. Wouldn't it take a long time to kill anyone in a fair-sized room with one of those small jets? Or would it? Certainly longer than if you had the oven turned on. Maybe it would take all night—but then, when I came to think of it, they had all night anyway. I wondered which room had been used. If the murderer had used his own then what did he do with himself all night? And why was there no smell of gas? Certainly, I had not smelled any. Perhaps somebody else had though. And if so, when? And where?

Barbara tried the door at that point, and I had to get up and let her in. She called me a sissy for locking it, but I told her she could expect to find it locked from then on—and I was quite prepared to call her a heroine if she were found murdered in her bed some morning.

"Did you talk to Dennis?" I asked.

She nodded. "You know, he's awfully nice. I mean—"

"Save it," I said coldly. "Did you find out what was scaring the Rostrums?"

"Well"—she shifted a bobby pin and curled up on the end of my bed—"Dennis got this letter, you see—they wrote him about once a month—just before he resigned from your father's canning factory."

"He was fired."

"Don't be silly!" Barbara said warmly. "He certainly—"

"Oh, all right—he walked out, leaving Papa in tears. Get on with it, can't you?"

She shifted the bobby pin again. "Where was I? Oh yes—Miss Opal said, in her letter, that she wanted some advice on a little matter that was bothering her, and then she went on to say that, as a matter of fact, it was frightening her. She could not put it down on paper and she did not want to confide in the Connecticut relatives because they had not been particularly friendly. But if Dennis would phone her the next time he came to New York she'd like to see him about this matter. Finally, she said the thing concerned one of the gentlemen in the house but she would not go further than that in a letter. And that was all."

"But what did she tell him when he got here?" I asked impatiently.

"Nothing to get excited about," she warned, shaking her head, "but it was curious, all the same. You see, when Dennis resigned from your father's factory and received the letter from Miss Opal, he decided to go to New York to arrange for a new position and he made up his mind to stay at Miss Opal's hotel. I guess he had a twinge of conscience about her, anyway, because she wrote to him regularly and he wrote to her when he thought of it, which was now and again. And he never did get around to paying her a visit. He says he hadn't seen her for years and years."

"Never mind going into his miserable conscience," I said, still impatient. "I know he's a snake. What did Opal tell him?"

"I'm getting to that," Barbara said calmly. "Dennis wrote to Miss Opal and said he was coming and told her about when he was due to arrive. When he got here Evie showed him to his room, and almost immediately there was a knock on the door, and Miss Opal slid in. He said she appeared to be in good spirits. She kissed him and asked him how he was and then said that she hadn't much time because she had to get back to her sister. Dennis asked why she hadn't brought her sister, but she said Imogene knew nothing about what was troubling her and she did not want her to know. She asked would Dennis please say nothing about being her godson. Nobody knew him, anyway, and he was to act as though they were strangers. As soon as she found an opportunity she would talk to him. And then she slid off."

"Is that all?" I asked, disappointed.

"Yep. He waited around for her to come and talk to him during the rest of that day and the next, but for some reason she never approached him. And then after dinner, on the second day, she and Miss Imogene disappeared. It seems he was quite upset and spent the next night making inquiries."

"Is that absolutely all?" I asked presently. "Are you sure you haven't left anything out?"

"Nope. Oh, there was one thing. Miss Opal told Dennis that before she talked to him she wanted to go upstairs and refer to her diary."

CHAPTER THIRTEEN

I STARED. "But listen—if Miss Opal talked to Dennis in his room, then her room would be downstairs, not upstairs."

But Barbara had evidently been through all that before. She yawned and murmured, "Somebody must have told you."

"The diary must be hidden up on the fourth floor," I persisted, beginning to get excited. "What's up there? Storeroom?"

Barbara yawned again and shook her head. "The storerooms are in the cellar. There are four small rooms upstairs. Evie and Kate share one; Uncle Alvin has one; Neville has one, and there's one vacant."

I sat up and swung my feet to the floor. "Barbara, we're wasting time. The solution to the whole thing must be in that diary. Let's go up and search."

She said, "There's no use in your getting into an uproar. Dennis had searched up there thoroughly, and of course he told the police about it, and Schmaltz has been tearing around there, too, but they couldn't find a thing. Schmaltz was simply raving. He says the diary must be found and acts as though we were all in a plot to keep it hidden from him."

I felt a bit damped but I said, "Let's go up and look around, anyway. We just might happen to find it, even if they didn't."

"Well, if you want to. But I don't think it's any use. Only we'd better wait until there's no one up there. I'll arrange it with Mama so that we can do it during dinner when we won't be interrupted."

I nodded and lowered myself onto the bed again. "Get her to keep something hot for us, and maybe she ought to pretend to be annoyed when we walk in late."

Barbara went off then, and I tried again to compose myself for sleep but I was interrupted almost immediately by Evie. She informed me, with a certain amount of manner, that Papa was receiving in his suite and would I come down at once. Only she pronounced it 'soot.'

I said, "No."

"No?" Evie repeated, astounded.

"No. Not even if he's receiving in his pajamas.'

Evie said practically, "What's his pajamas got to do with it? He wants you right away and he's gonna be mad if you don't come."

I rolled over and closed my eyes.

"Stroke his hair and chuck him under the chin," I said sleepily. "He'll be all right."

I heard Evie say, "Not me. I'm gonna run when I tell him what you said," and then I slipped off into a sound sleep.

I was rudely awakened by Papa, himself, bursting into my room. I opened one eye and muttered, "I knew there'd be some rubbish drifting in here. I forgot to lock the door."

"You mind your manners," Papa said furiously. "And the next time I send for you you're to come, understand?"

"Not while you aren't supporting me, I won't," I said, opening the other eye.

He detoured into a vigorous dissertation on the foolishness and danger of leaving money to brainless young girls. I was nearly asleep again when he at last got back to the point.

"As a matter of fact, I want to have a serious talk with you."

"All right," I said, "sit down and have it. If it's interesting it might even keep me awake."

He sat down and beetled his brows. "Now, listen. I want you to stay away from that Livingstone fellow. I know he'd like to marry you so that he could get an in at the factory, and I don't want him. In fact, I'm telling you now—and you'd better remember it—that I won't have him, no matter what the circumstances."

"Suppose I fall in love with him?" I said reasonably. "You can't let your own son-in-law lean on a shovel for a living."

"Not at all," said Papa nastily. "You can support him by playing Juliet—or little Eva. Not to mention your own private income that you've been waving under my nose."

I sat up and glared at him. I was so mad that I got a bit mixed up and thought for a moment that I was actually in love with Dennis and wanted to marry him. "If you think you can step in with your moneybags and crush the love of two—"

"Save it for the footlights," said Papa rudely. "And remember, I will not give my consent to a marriage with that pup. So you'd better bear in mind what I've been saying."

He got up to go, and I asked, "What room are you in?"

"Second-floor front," he barked.

I said, "Oh yes, that big one. It's so expensive that it's mostly vacant. Mrs. Markham waits—and prays—for a sucker like you to take it."

"I've been called a lot of harsh things in my time," said Papa, pausing by the door, "but neither friend nor enemy has ever called me a sucker."

"Well, listen—may I have some of the girls in your room for cocktails at about six o'clock? I owe a bit of entertainment here and there."

He came back into the room. "Certainly, quite all right as far as I'm concerned. Only it isn't quite seemly to have a party at this time."

"No," I admitted. "But I want to get them together so that I can ask a few questions."

"You leave all that to Schmaltz," he said firmly.

"Yes, but you see, I'm on the inside working out, and he's on the outside working in."

"And when you meet the thing will be solved," Papa suggested, polishing up his sarcasm.

I said, "That's very funny."

He left me then and pounded down the stairs, making enough noise to wake Uncle Alvin, who was undoubtedly taking his nap on the fourth floor.

I gave up any hope of further sleep and decided to go down and see if Mary and Grace had returned from school yet.

I went down to the front hall and ran across Schmaltz and a couple of his playmates. I tried to duck, but Schmaltz caught me, and I was led away and questioned until I was dizzy. Camille came wandering up after a while, and while they captured her I made my escape.

I went back to the second floor and, hearing voices in Mary's room, I knocked and walked in. Mary, Grace, and Dennis were sitting around, apparently having a comfortable chat.

I was a bit taken aback when I saw Dennis, and I stood in silence while they all looked at me expectantly.

"Are you looking for me?" Dennis asked at last.

I said, "Naturally. Who else?"

"Come on, Diana," Grace said impatiently, "What is it?"

"I want you to come in and meet my father," I said, feeling a bit self-conscious, "and have a drink."

"How old is he?" Mary asked.

"Mary!" Grace yipped. "What's the matter with you? Take a chance."

"Thanks very much," Dennis said. "We accept with pleasure."

"You mean you're coming too?" I asked doubtfully.

"Oh yes," he said easily. "I'm a democratic soul, and besides, the girls need an escort."

"It's all right with me," I said, "because I'm democratic too. But I think Papa might throw you out. Anyway, I'll see you in ten minutes in the luxury suite."

I left them and hurried downstairs. Camille was still in the drawing room with Schmaltz, so I crept past quietly and went on to the kitchen.

I found Barbara there and, ignoring Kate and Evie, I went over and whispered into her ear. "Did you fix it with your mother for us to be late for dinner?"

Barbara nodded, and Kate snapped. "Ma woulda boxed my ears for whispering in front of folks when I was a young 'un."

"Quite right too," Barbara agreed primly.

"All right," I said loudly. "I merely want some liquor sent to Papa's room and charged on his bill."

"I'm afraid that would be illegal," Barbara said. "We have no license. But I'll give you some scotch if you like."

I said, "Thanks, I would like. And don't forget 'extras' or 'misc' when you come to make out Papa's bill."

She produced the scotch and some soda and ice, and I invited her to come and join us. She said she'd run up just before dinner.

Camille was emerging from the drawing room as I passed through the hall, and without a word she followed me up and right into Papa's room. "Somebody throwing a little party?" she asked brightly.

Papa glanced at the scotch and said that if there was going to be any drinking he thought he'd better go.

"No, you don't," I said. "I want you to meet my friends."

He said all right, he'd meet them but he'd have to go after that. He took a bottle and started to open it, and I offered Camille a drink. She said she never drank but she'd like to stay and chat for a while.

Mary and Grace came in, followed by Dennis, who tried to shut the door behind him but was balked by an obstruction which turned out to be Miss Giddens. She gave Dennis a look of reproof and then walked straight up to Papa and peered into his face.

Papa backed away and said helplessly, "Diana, try and control your girlfriend."

Camille brushed Miss Giddens to one side, which gave Papa a free view of Dennis. He roared, "For God's sake! Is this monkey one of your girlfriends?"

"Shut up, Papa!" I said out of the corner of my mouth. "Try and be cultured for once."

I introduced him to Mary and Grace, and he appeared to be quite charmed with them and stopped fussing with Dennis. I handed the drinks around and gave Miss Giddens plain soda. She sniffed at it, took a sip, sneezed, and emptied the entire glassful onto Papa's bed. He didn't see her, so I didn't bother to tell him about it.

I took my own drink to a quiet corner, and Dennis followed me. He rested one hand on the back of my chair and, leaning over me in a properly attentive attitude, started a line of conversation that was shot with sparkle, whimsey, and several other things.

"You're wasting your time," I told him. "Papa's too busy showing off to Mary and Grace to notice."

He straightened up and said it was a good thing I'd told him because his back was aching and it was just a good posture gone to waste.

Mary and Grace presently disentangled themselves from Papa, with some valuable help from Camille, and came over to surround Dennis. They noticed me long enough to suggest that I refill their glasses.

I attended to them and then went to get another drink for Papa. He thanked me by giving me a baleful look and snarling in what was supposed to be a whisper, "If you don't take this blasted Mack Sennett bathing beauty off my neck I'll marry her to get even with you."

"Go ahead," I said carelessly. "She's just about your age and a perfect match for that house you built. It would be very suitable."

I wandered around for a while and then tried to insinuate myself in between Mary and Grace, but they merely handed me their glasses, which were empty again, and I had to go back and fill them. When I returned they accepted the drinks and then closed up tightly, leaving me on the outside of the circle.

I saw Papa get rid of Camille by the simple expedient of walking away from her, and he went straight over and bullied his way in between Mary and Grace, which brought him face to face with Dennis. Dennis was in the middle of a long, boring story about how he had talked himself out of a ticket after going through a red light, and he merely raised his voice a couple of notches and kept right on with it. Papa, of course, never had time for other people's stories, so he opened up with a loud bellow on one of his own.

Mary and Grace began to giggle helplessly, and Miss Giddens padded over and stared first at Papa and then at Dennis.

Papa was the first to give up. He backed away from Miss Giddens' peering shoe-button eyes and roared, "Livingstone! Stop wasting your confounded breath and do your duty by the ladies. Miss—er—Giddens has no drink."

Dennis had got to that breathless point in his story where he informed the cop that his mother, the late Mrs. Livingstone, had been born Maggie Murphy. However, he stopped, raised his eyebrows, and said he hoped he was still a gentleman. He took Miss Giddens by the arm, said, "Come on, honey bun, let's get another drink," and marched her off. Camille shrieked with laughter and said, "I'll fix you up," and began to fuss with the bottles and ice.

Mary and Grace decided that they needed another drink, too, so they took hold of Papa and ran him over to the table. They all started to talk at once, then, and I realized that they were well on the way to being drunk and disorderly. I kept myself apart and stayed sober because I felt that Barbara and I had serious business afoot.

She came in just as Papa and Dennis were raising their glasses to each other. Papa said, "A row of brick houses! And I hope one of them falls on you." And at the same time Dennis murmured politely, "To crime! And your close and skillful connection therewith."

"What's going on?" Barbara asked, frowning. "I hope they're not going to fight."

"It's all right," I assured her. "They're quite peaceful, really."

"Well, let's break it up, anyhow. The dinner gong just went."

The breaking up wasn't so easy, except for Miss Giddens, who departed at once. It took about fifteen minutes of steady work to get the others out onto the landing and five more before they were well started down the stairs. Grace simplified it by sliding down the banisters—which would have been all right except that it ended in a curve instead of a newel post, and she went right on to the hall floor. She tried to insist that she was badly injured, but the others told her to think nothing of it and took her, limping, into the dinning room.

As soon as they were out of sight Barbara and I hurried up to the fourth floor.

"We'll go to the vacant room first," Barbara decided. "It was never rented, and I think it's the most likely place for her to have hidden it.

Although why she couldn't have hidden it in her own room beats me."

"But she was trying to keep it a secret from Miss Imogene," I explained eagerly. "She wouldn't even let Dennis make himself known to Miss Imogene for fear she'd know something was doing, since he never visited them."

Barbara said, "Uh-huh," absentmindedly and opened the door to the vacant room. She stopped with a little gasp, and I looked over her shoulder.

The room was in utter confusion. It had been practically torn to pieces, with the curtains ripped from the windows and lying on the floor, and the mattress half off the bed. All the drawers of the bureau were hanging open.

We stood there for a moment, gaping at the wreck, and then suddenly, behind us, someone let out a shrill, hysterical laugh.

CHAPTER FOURTEEN

WE BOTH SWUNG AROUND and came face to face with Camille, who stared at us with a peculiar glazed look about her eyes.

Barbara recovered herself at once and, taking Camille's arm, said persuasively, "Wouldn't you be better in your own room?"

Camille jerked her arm away, and her face reddened with sudden anger. "Leave me alone. What are you doing here, snooping into other people's affairs? Why don't you mind your own business?"

Barbara dropped the persuasive note and said more firmly, "If you won't come to your room I'll have to call Mama."

Camille lowered her eyes, and her face became sulky. She gave a little hiccough and, turning away, made a lurch for the stairs. Barbara went after her and, with a steady arm about her waist, helped her to go down.

I realized, with some astonishment, that she was drunk and I wondered how on earth she had managed to get that way. The last time I had noticed her was when she was on her way down to dinner with the others, but she must have turned around in the dining room and come straight up again. I remembered that she had refused when I had offered her a drink, but when I came to think of it she had been standing near the table where the liquor was and had even helped me to pour out a couple. I supposed that she had been quietly helping herself and, once started on the stuff, was unable to call a halt.

Barbara got her to her room and onto her bed and then came out and closed the door so firmly that it banged.

"There!" she said. "Damn it! I wish I lived all alone even if it was in a hole in the wall."

We hurried back upstairs and went into Neville's room. As I had expected it was in apple-pie order, with not so much as a pin out of place. It made our search a good deal easier, and we went through every article he owned, but there was no diary, and the only thing we found that was of any interest was a pair of corsets.

Barbara tossed them back into the drawer and said scornfully, "The conceited old fool!"

"Not at all," I said reasonably. "He has as much right to appear at his best as you have."

We finished Neville's room and went on to Evie's and Kate's, which was the oddest-looking room I'd ever seen. There was a broad white chalk line running down the center of the floor, and on each side was a bed, bureau, and chair. One side was neat and clean, the other dusty and untidy with the bed unmade.

"Easy to tell which is which," Barbara said, giggling. "Kate is the tidy one."

We tackled Evie's side first, because it was the more difficult, and then ran through Kate's things. We did find a diary, as it happened, but it was Kate's. It was a large, thick book, and we decided to read a little of it, just in case it might be Miss Opal's diary in disguise. We opened at a spot where Kate was in her thirties, and found it very hard to stop. The revelations were such as to make Evie's little goings on sound like a tame canary.

"And the way she sniffs at Evie doing a little innocent dancing!" Barbara said in amazement.

We closed the book when Kate reached forty—not because it was boring but because our consciences were beginning to bother us a trifle.

The delay made it too late for Uncle Alvin's room, for we heard him coming up the stairs when we got out into the hall. We hid in the vacant room while he passed on to his own, and Barbara whispered, "We haven't really looked in here yet."

"What's the use?" I asked, glancing around at the confusion. "It's already been done."

"How do you know? Maybe whoever wrecked it was looking for something else. I guess you and Dennis and I are the only ones who know about the diary."

"You left out the entire police force," I reminded her.

"Oh, well—yes," she admitted. "I suppose Schmaltz made all this mess then."

"No," I said doubtfully. "Somehow, I think the police do better and cleaner searching than this."

We had a quick look around but found nothing and presently we went on downstairs. We agreed not to give up but to search the fourth floor again. "Only we'd better make sure that the police haven't found it in the meantime," Barbara said sensibly.

The dining room was nearly deserted. Mrs. Markham was still there, and Papa, and they were exchanging courteous remarks across the room to each other.

I sat down with Papa, and he said, "It's nice of you to spare me a little of your time at dinner. Where the devil have you been?"

"I had a run in my stocking," I said briefly and started in on the soup.

"And maybe you had to darn a hole in your garter belt," he said furiously. "What's a run in your stocking got to do with your being three quarters of an hour late for dinner while I eat alone? D'ya think I'm a fool?"

"Don't tempt me," I said, still scooping up the soup.

He got a little melancholy over me at that point. "All the money," he said wistfully, "that I spent on your education. I don't regret the kindergarten fees, but after that it was a dead loss."

I said, "Hush. You'll have Mrs. Markham and Barbara splitting their sides."

He waited until I had finished and then escorted me to the drawing room. Dodd and Schmaltz were not in evidence, and when Mrs. Markham came in, after a few minutes, I asked her if they'd gone off for a holiday.

"Oh, they'll be back," she said with a resigned little sigh. "They're never absent for very long. You know, they searched every room in the house, and of course I was obliged to help them. They did it more or less secretly—I suppose so that people would be taken unaware, and before they could hide things. It was really very embarrassing for me. But I believe Inspector Dodd quite fancies himself as a detective—and that Schmaltz toadies to him."

"Did they find anything?" I asked eagerly.

She shook her head doubtfully. "If you mean the diary, I don't know, but I don't believe they found anything that was of any value to them. I know I heard Schmaltz complaining about the lack of clues."

Barbara joined us just then and said in a low voice, "We must find out whether Schmaltz found that diary, and then when we get a chance we'll do Uncle Alvin's room."

"I don't like it," Mrs. Markham said in a bothered voice. "I don't like to see you girls interfering in such a serious business. Really, much as I want the thing cleared up I'd rather you didn't get into any sort of trouble."

"It's all right, Mama," Barbara soothed her. "We're not doing anything that can land us in trouble."

"I'm worried about that room that was torn apart," Mrs. Markham said after a slight pause. "I know that the police did not leave it that way, for I was up on the fourth floor when they searched it and I saw each of those rooms when they had finished, and you would never have known that anyone had been there."

"I wonder who did it then " Barbara mused

"Camille, maybe," I suggested. "She was drunk and she came right up after us and told us to stop snooping."

Barbara nodded. "You're going to look in on Camille, anyway, aren't you, Mama? Why don't you try to get out of her whether she messed that room up or not, and if she did, perhaps you can find out what she was looking for."

"All right, I will," Mrs. Markham said with sudden decision, "if you'll promise me to keep out of mischief tonight. Go to bed early and don't do any more snooping."

Barbara agreed, and Mrs. Markham went off. I turned around and found that I had Miss Giddens at my elbow. She blinked her beady little eyes at me and mumbled, "I want to tell you—" and was immediately drowned out by Papa, who asked me in a friendly roar if I would make a fourth at bridge with Mary, Grace, and himself.

"No," I said, "I won't."

"You'll have to," he boomed. "There's no one else, and these ladies claim to be a pair of experts and declare that they can take us over."

"You know perfectly well," I said, "that I swore off being your partner the last time I played with you when you—"

"Quiet," said Papa, lowering his voice. "It'll be all right this time, I assure you."

I shook my head mutely.

"Bribe?" he said, lowering his voice still further.

"One hundred dollars cash in advance," I told him, beginning to brighten up.

I glanced around to wink at Barbara, but she had gone. Miss Giddens was still at my elbow, staring into my face and moving her lips. Dennis and Neville were not in sight, and Uncle Alvin had evidently stayed in his room. Grace and Mary were looking at me expectantly.

"Where is everybody?" I asked. "Papa uses the right soap and tooth powder, so it can't be that."

Papa eased over to me and tried to push a small roll of bills into my hand, but I knew it couldn't be as much as a hundred. "Not enough," I said coldly and turned back to Mary and Grace. "Why has everyone disappeared?" I persisted.

Mary shrugged. "We don't know, and personally, I don't care."

"I'll bet you know where Dennis is."

"Business appointment," said Grace glibly.

"Here's your damned money," Papa whispered, and this time the roll looked all right, so I accepted it.

Miss Giddens spoke up suddenly and quite clearly. "You see, I am to have another visitor tomorrow—but I must not tell anyone."

CHAPTER FIFTEEN

THERE WAS A SMALL SILENCE, and then Grace shuddered and cried out with a touch of hysteria, "What does she mean? What is she talking about?"

"Shut up, Grace!" Mary said sharply. "What's the matter with you, anyway?"

"Who told you that you were going to have another visitor?" I asked Miss Giddens as gently as I could.

The old lady gave a satisfied nod and said, "Yes."

"Yes, what?" Papa roared, spoiling everything.

Miss Giddens took fright, of course, and after a startled look at him she scuttled over to the window and stood there, clutching at the lace curtains.

"Come on," Mary said impatiently, "let's get this game started if we're ever going to."

While they were fussing with cards and ashtrays and the table, I walked quietly over to Miss Giddens. "May I come tomorrow, too—and see your visitor?" I asked in a low voice.

"Yes, certainly. Very pleased, I'm sure. But you must not tell anyone."

"Why not?"

"Eh?" said the old lady vaguely.

"Why can't I tell anyone?"

"No, no. You must not."

"Did the gentleman say you must not tell?" I asked hopefully.

She made no reply.

Papa peremptorily ordered me to the bridge table at that point, so I gave it up.

We settled down to play, and I realized right from the start that my mind was not on the game. I made several determined efforts to concentrate, but they were all failures.

Miss Giddens, always attracted by cards, presently drifted over and established herself beside me on the couch. It made things more difficult, because I knew she had to be watched, since she had a habit of quietly removing a card or two and slipping them into her pocket or down the front of her dress.

My mind wandered off into speculation as to how I could find out about her secret visitor, and Papa started first to grumble and then to bellow. I had a vague idea that his complaints were justified, but they rose to such volume that they presently produced Mrs. Markham. She made a request, iced all around with formal courtesy, that we play more quietly, since she could hear us from her bedroom on the third floor.

Papa nodded with offended dignity and agreed to soft pedal, and when Mrs. Markham had gone he made some ridiculous statement about the walls and fussy people and the lack of consideration shown to a man who never raised his voice above a whisper, anyway.

Shortly after that I found myself in favor again. I don't know just what I did but I came out of my abstraction to find the three of them glowing with admiration.

"I have always said that Diana had the makings of a bridge player," Papa conceded.

Five minutes later we found that we had played several hands with four cards missing.

"I thought you told me you were a bunch of first-class players," I said politely. "A beginner like myself could not be expected to notice, but—"

"Oh, turn it off," said Mary impatiently. "Search the old lady and get them back."

"No," I said, eying Miss Giddens' various bits of old clothing. "I don't want to search her." However, I turned to her and asked if she could lend us some cards, as we hadn't enough.

Miss Giddens took it under consideration and presently produced the four missing cards. "But I must ask you to return them to me," she said with quiet dignity.

"At the earliest opportunity," I promised. "Thank you kindly."

Dennis walked in at that point. He joined us without a flicker of embarrassment and arranged himself comfortably on the couch—which had me squeezed in between him and Miss Giddens.

Papa glared at him, but Dennis kept his eyes on Grace and Mary. "You don't mind if I watch?"

Grace and Mary did not mind and said so with such enthusiasm that Papa had to put a series of sneering remarks back onto the stove and let them simmer. In the end he said almost mildly, "You'll find it more interesting if you watch one of the other hands. My daughter is the weak player here."

"Thanks," said Dennis, "but I prefer to watch a weak player. It gives me a pleasant sense of superiority."

Papa, frustrated above the table, evidently kicked out below it to relieve his feelings and apparently caught Grace on the shin. In the ensuing jumble of apologies and assurances which Grace gave through clenched teeth I turned to Dennis and asked him, in a low voice, if Miss Opal's diary had been found, either by himself or the police.

He frowned and asked sharply, "What do you know about it?"

I explained that Barbara and I worked together and kept each other's secrets.

"I told Barbara about it," he said slowly, "because I thought she might be able to locate it. But apparently she's as much in the dark as anyone else."

"Then the police haven't found it?"

He shook his head. "They questioned me about it again after they had searched and just didn't call me a liar. But they said rather pointedly that if she had had a diary they would have found it."

"That's sour grapes," I said scornfully. "The Rostrums were just the type to keep diaries. They hadn't much else to do."

He nodded. "They found Miss Imogene's, but I understand that hers had nothing much more than the weather in it."

"Well, that's what you'd expect," I said thoughtfully. "And you'd think Miss Opal's would be like that too."

"Diana!" Papa roared. "We're all waiting for you."

I hastily gathered up my cards and spread them out and then I felt a surge of anger at Papa for having interrupted my train of thought by intruding his miserable bridge.

"Three no trump!" I yelled.

Dennis hissed air in through his teeth, and Grace said, "Double," in a quiet, ladylike manner.

"Redouble!" Papa shouted.

I looked at my hand then and found that I held a jack and two tens, outside of the rubbish.

"Excuse me," I said, rising hastily. "Will you play it, Papa? I must wash my hands."

I laid my cards face down on the table and made off. I heard Mary trying to combine courtesy with a remark to the effect that it was not quite fair, but Papa was beaming, and I knew he was confident that his expert handling could wring out a couple of overtricks.

I was halfway up the first flight of stairs when I heard his cry of anguish and I ran all the rest of the way to my room.

I found Barbara lying on my bed, reading my diary, and I snatched it away from her.

"That's a very low thing to do," I said coldly.

"Why?" she asked, opening her eyes very wide. "As a matter of fact, it's quite interesting. Only I don't understand why you didn't marry that Count X. He sounds absolutely fascinating, and yet you turned him down."

I turned away to the mirror and murmured, "I didn't want him," which wasn't exactly true. But since Count X was nothing but my imagination I couldn't have had him anyway.

Barbara lay and watched me make up my face, and after a while she said, "The police have all gone—not one left. So we're alone with the murderer."

"For God's sake, Barbara," I whispered, "don't gloat over it."

"I'm not gloating," she said soberly. "I'm scared stiff. If I could think of any reason for those two poor creatures to be killed I wouldn't be so frightened. But it sounds like a maniac who kills for the pleasure of killing, and then wraps them up in the portieres and puts one in Miss Giddens' room. He thinks that's funny, so he puts the other one out on the seat on the balcony."

She started to shiver so violently that it rattled the bed, and I stamped my foot at her. "Stop being silly and come downstairs with me. We'll make some strong coffee."

She pulled herself off the bed and shook her head as though to clear it. "I've been in this room alone too long, I guess. Even when you came up I held my breath and wondered whether it was someone with an ax over his shoulder. That's why I read your diary—to try and take my mind off the thing."

We went on down, and on the second floor I cautioned Barbara to be quiet. "I did something to Papa that he won't get over for a while and I don't want to be caught and punished."

When we reached the front hall we could hear Papa and Dennis both talking at the same time and, to my astonishment, they both sounded amiable.

The portieres had not been replaced, and I urged Barbara toward the bare arch. "See what's going on," I whispered.

She peered in cautiously and then came back and gave me the picture. "Dennis and your father are playing partners, and they must have struck oil because they're both complementing themselves on their own thoughtful bids. Mary and Grace are just sitting there, and it's a good thing they don't have gills, else they'd be green around them."

"There's always a fly in every ointment," I said, sighing. "Mary and Grace were badly in need of a taking over at bridge, but I'd rather see anyone do it than Papa and Dennis."

We went to the kitchen, where we found Miss Giddens poking into various drawers and cupboards.

"The poor old soul is hungry," Barbara said. "I'll get her some cookies."

She produced some keys and unlocked the pantry. "We have to keep this stuff locked up," she explained with a faint note of apology. "Otherwise, we wouldn't make any money. We can't lock the ice box, naturally."

"Of course," I said, "I understand. You can put this on Papa's bill. Supper for daughter."

"Oh no—certainly not," Barbara said and handed Miss Giddens the cookies. The old lady grabbed at them and shuffled hastily out of the kitchen as though she were afraid they were going to be snatched away again.

We made the coffee, and after a while Uncle Alvin wandered in.

"Hello," he said amiably, "I thought I smelled coffee. Might I have a cup, if it's no trouble?"

Barbara said, "Of course," and went to the cupboard for another cup. She poured some coffee and handed it to him, and he looked at her with an affectionate little smile.

My eyes happened to be on his face, and I saw the smile freeze suddenly and his whole expression become rigid. The cup and saucer fell from his hand and crashed onto the floor.

CHAPTER SIXTEEN

BARBARA BACKED AWAY a step, and her face paled. "What—what is it?" she stammered. "What's wrong with me? Why are you staring?"

But Uncle Alvin had pulled himself together. He knelt down and began to pick up the pieces of the shattered cup. "I'm sorry, dear—it's nothing. I had a bit of a turn. If you'll pour me some more coffee I shall be all right."

"Do you feel ill?" I asked, and he murmured, "A little."

I went to the cupboard for a fresh cup and poured the coffee while he tidily disposed of the broken china. Barbara continued to watch him, and presently she spoke in a low, earnest voice. "Uncle Alvin, I wish you'd tell me what it is. The Rostrums stared at me like that, too, and— and then they both died. What did you see? Please tell me—I'm scared."

He sat down to his coffee and gave her a reassuring little smile. "You must not let your imagination run away with you, Barbara. I guess we're all a little on edge, but we must try and keep our feet on the ground. I had a queer turn—that's all. I expect I strained myself a bit today—I dug that tulip bed out again. They had simply shoveled the dirt back in any old way, so I got it all out again and sorted the bulbs. I intend to put them in properly, first thing in the morning—but I've been a bit worried about leaving that great hole out there in the darkness. I hope no one goes wandering out there and stumbling in."

Barbara impatiently brushed the tulips and their bed to one side. "Uncle Alvin, if you know anything please don't keep it a secret like—like they did. It might not be safe—something might happen to you."

He showed a touch of impatience himself. "Don't be silly, child. I'm not as young as I was and I'm apt to get these turns occasionally. I'll be as right as rain in the morning."

"What kind of a turn was it?" Barbara asked, still trying to pin him down.

He finished his coffee and got up from the table. "Dizziness—a little vertigo. I think I'll go to my room now."

"Wait!" Barbara said frantically. "Don't go." But Uncle Alvin murmured, "Good night," and shuffled off.

Barbara dropped heavily into a chair and looked at me. "What on earth do you make of it?"

I was completely mystified and I told her so.

"I don't see how it can be anything but coincidence, Barbara," I said after a moment.

She shook her head. "It can't be coincidence."

"Then, what is it?"

She frowned faintly and compressed her lips but she had nothing to offer.

We drank coffee in silence for a while, and then I was hit by a rather terrifying thought.

"Listen, Barbara—Miss Giddens announced this evening that she was to have a visitor tomorrow. Remember, the Rostrums stared at you in that funny way, and then Miss Giddens had visitors—and the Rostrums died. Uncle Alvin looked at you queerly tonight—and Miss Giddens expects a visitor tomorrow. Maybe it doesn't mean a thing, and I'm just being silly— but somehow, I think we ought to watch Uncle Alvin. Follow him around and keep him in sight as much as possible—at least tonight and tomorrow."

"Maybe we'd better," she agreed nervously. "I guess we're being dopey—but it won't do any harm." She piled the coffee cups in the sink, and I could see that her teeth were chattering.

We went through to the front hall and were about to climb the stairs when we heard Uncle Alvin's voice from the direction of the drawing room. We changed our course and took a look.

The bridge game was still alive, with Papa and Dennis still playing partners. Miss Giddens had disappeared, and Uncle Alvin sat on the couch where she had been.

Barbara and I glanced at each other and then walked straight in and established ourselves on the couch beside Dennis. Uncle Alvin peered around him from the other side and asked mildly, "Hadn't you girls better go to bed?"

"Certainly they should go to bed," Mary said crisply. "Children need more sleep than adults."

Papa raised his head and noticed me for the first time. "Oh, it's you. That was a clever trick you pulled—that three no trump. Going off and dumping it in my lap . . ."

"How many did you go down?" I asked indifferently.

Dennis said, "Be quiet. I'm trying to concentrate."

Everybody shut up, including even Papa, and Dennis finished playing the hand in a dead silence. It turned out to be the end of a rubber, and they decided to settle up and go to bed.

We all went upstairs together. Mary, Grace, and Papa said good night all around on the second floor, and the rest of us climbed to the third, where Alvin said good night and wended his way up to the fourth. I watched him for a moment, still panting myself, and thought it would be only reasonable if he did have a touch of heart trouble and maybe Barbara and I were acting like a couple of kids.

Barbara, Dennis, and I separated to our rooms, but I merely walked in, turned around, and came out again. I went to the foot of the stairs leading to the fourth floor and decided to wait there for Barbara. I knew I'd have to wait because she never could go into her room without powdering her nose whether it needed it or not. I could not help thinking of my bed, and yet I was glad we had decided to watch over Uncle Alvin, even if it was silly.

A door opened abruptly, but it turned out to be Dennis, instead of Barbara. There was nowhere to hide, even if I'd had time, and he saw me at once. He said, "Psst."

I tried to ignore him, but somehow, the next thing I knew I was sitting in the armchair in his room, and he was pouring out a drink that looked like Mary's brand of port.

"What do you want?" I asked crossly. "I haven't time to be fooling here with you."

"Why? I'm quite a nice little boy when you really know me. Went to the right school, know the right people, and do the right things."

"You don't work in the right factory is the only trouble, I guess."

He said, "Don't get to be like your father."

"What's the matter with Papa?" I asked hotly.

"I don't know," said Dennis. "I've often wondered. Some perfectly simple explanation, no doubt, if we could but find it."

"I'm going," I said, getting up. "I oughtn't to be here, anyway. It isn't conventional."

He pushed me back into the chair and asked, "What dark business have you on tonight that keeps you so busy you can't stay and play for a while?"

"Whatever it is," I said coldly, "it doesn't concern you."

"I hardly hoped that it would. But on the other hand, it's early—barely twelve—and I'd like to talk to you."

At that moment I distinctly heard Barbara come out of her room and creak around toward the stairs, and I supposed she was under the impression that she hadn't made a sound.

I rose hastily and made for the door, but Dennis got there before me. He opened it, stuck his head out, and called in a stage whisper, "Barbara!"

I saw her come toward us slowly with her eyebrows up in her hair somewhere.

"Can you get along without sis, here?" Dennis asked.

"She promised to stay and keep me company if she could get away from you."

"It's a lie! I did not!" I hissed in a whisper that vibrated around the hall. They said "Shh."

"It's quite all right," Barbara added. "It's just a small chore, and I can do it myself." She made for the stairs again, and I could see that she was a little offended.

"I'll be right up," I whispered after her.

But Dennis closed the door and pushed me back to the armchair. "You girls shouldn't spend all your time in pairs—it spoils your chances. You don't want to be an old maid, do you?"

"It sounds very nice and peaceful," I said crossly. "What do you want with me anyway? I have to go."

"Not yet—I want to find out what you're like. After all, your father practically handed you to me on a platter. I merely want to see what I turned down—and I've had a devil of a time getting you alone."

"Well, take a good look," I said, smoothing down my dress. "Aren't you sorry now? Am I not beautiful? And rich too. And there you sit—just one of Papa's ex-canners. Opportunity knocked—but you listened to the voice of pride instead."

He nodded. "All wrong—I can see that now. I've been offered another position, but it isn't as good as the old one in your father's slave mill. The only way I can get that back, as far as I can see, is to make up to you and work myself into the old man's good graces."

"You don't see very far then," I said scornfully. "He warned me to keep away from you."

"Oh well—I expected that. But I've paved the way by playing good bridge with him. Even he must see that if I marry you I'll be doing him two good turns at once. I lure you away from your career, and he gets a good bridge player into the family—which is a mighty important thing to him."

I stood up and moved toward the door. "I'll fall in with your plans and marry you and all that if you'll agree to a few trifling conditions. You must play bridge with Papa whenever he feels like it. You must take entire charge of our children because I'm going on with my career, in any case, and won't have the time, and of course I can't live in upstate New York. But you may come and visit me when it's convenient."

Dennis opened the door for me. "The conditions are a little tough—and I had not exactly made up my mind about marrying you as yet—but I'll give the whole thing my best attention and let you know."

I said, "Right," and, slipping out, closed the door in his face.

I crept cautiously up to the fourth floor and felt all around the landing for Barbara but I could not find her and I was afraid to speak. I went back to the stairs and, leaning over the banister, I looked down into the stair well. It was faintly lighted by a pair of long windows that rose from the turn in the stairs to the level of the floor above. I found myself looking at the windows with a queer, uneasy sense of something wrong.

And then I got it. One of a pair of heavy side drapes that ordinarily hung there was missing.

CHAPTER SEVENTEEN

I DREW IN MY BREATH sharply and continued to stare through the darkness at the semi-denuded windows. There was no doubt about it—one of the drapes had disappeared and, with sudden rising terror, I whirled around and began to search frantically around the black hallway for Barbara. She had preceded me by only a few minutes, and I was sure that she must be up there somewhere. There was not a sound of any kind, but I could see a thin glow of light under Uncle Alvin's door and under the bathroom door.

I had an impulse to turn and run back to my room—or even to Dennis' room—but I checked it because I felt that I ought to locate Barbara first. I decided, to the accompaniment of my chattering teeth, that I had better look in the vacant room, as that seemed the most likely place for her to be. I began to move quietly in that direction, but at the same time Uncle Alvin's door opened soundlessly, and Barbara peered out. I gave a little gasp of relief and hurried over to her, and she pulled me into the room. "Quick!" she hissed. "If we're going to watch over him we'd better hide in here."

"Where is he?" I whispered.

"In the bathroom. Stop wasting time and find somewhere to hide."

I looked around the bare little room and said, "Don't be silly—you couldn't hide a can of peas here. We'll go into that vacant room and then we can see, or at least hear, if anyone goes by."

She agreed somewhat reluctantly, and we tiptoed out of Uncle Alvin's room. As we left my eye happened to fall upon one of his books, and it was titled *Elsie Dinsmore.*

We made the spare room without mishap and sat down on the bed.

"This isn't half as good as being right in there with him," Barbara pouted.

"You should go at things with more finesse," I said reprovingly. "We'd merely be discovered at once, and what good would that do? Your mother would be angry, and we'd be sent straight to bed."

"It's probably where we ought to be," she said huffily. "What are we doing sitting here in the dark, anyway?"

"I guess we should have got in touch with the police and told them all we know," I agreed soberly.

"We could go down and phone them now," she said, and I could feel her shivering. "And something might happen to Uncle Alvin in the meantime."

I whispered, "That's what we're doing, sitting here. We're waiting for someone to come and murder Uncle Alvin."

"Oh, don't!" she moaned. "Why would anyone murder him? What has he ever done?"

"What did the Rostrums ever do?"

"Yes, I know," she muttered gloomily.

I told her about the drape then, and she became very excited. She knew nothing about its having been removed for any domestic reason and was sure, in that case, that they would both have been taken down anyway. In the midst of our feverish, whispered discussion we heard Uncle Alvin come out of the bathroom, and we left the bed and flew to the door to listen.

He went straight to his room, and we heard the door close firmly.

We returned to the bed and sat for a while in gloomy silence. Presently I asked listlessly "Barbara, why has your uncle a copy of *Elsie Dinsmore* among his books? Don't tell me he reads it."

"Why not?" she asked. "I did."

"Well, yes, but I don't suppose you have it now. I mean, in full view among the books in your bedroom."

She said, "Of course I haven't, and I don't believe Uncle Alvin has either. You've been seeing things."

"I haven't. And he has," I said shortly.

"He isn't the type at all," Barbara said reasonably. "He's interested in gardening and walks and fixing the kitchen doorknob and reading long, historical novels."

"I'll prove it to you the next time we get a chance," I said indifferently.

Someone came out of one of the rooms at that point, and we went silently to the door again to listen. Barbara opened it a crack, so that we could see as well.

It was Uncle Alvin, and this time he went straight down the stairs. We allowed him to get out of sight and then we followed on tiptoes.

On the third floor the light was burning in the hall, although it had been out when I had gone up. It was supposed to burn all night but it was out very often, and I suspected Mrs. Markham of sneaking out and turning it off to save on the electric bills. Grace had said that boardinghouse keepers were apt to get that way.

The light made it very obvious that Uncle Alvin was not in the hall, so we walked around and listened at the various doors in case he might be talking to someone. All was quiet, however, except in Dennis' room. Dennis was snoring.

"That settles it," I said. "I'd never marry a man who snores."

"Hopeless," Barbara agreed, shaking her head. "Whoever would have suspected it?"

We looked in our own rooms and the bathroom, but they were empty, so we went on down to the second floor.

The hall was deserted, and there was absolute silence from Grace's and Mary's rooms. Papa was snoring with even more vim than Dennis.

"Your mother wasn't so particular," Barbara commented.

"I beg your pardon," I said formally, "but my mother lived in an age when it was not possible to determine these things before marriage. In other words, she was hooked."

We looked in the bathroom and found no one and then we went on to Miss Giddens' room, where we walked straight in without bothering to knock. She must have been awake because she got out of bed at once and turned on the light.

"Make yourselves at home, ladies," she said politely. "May I offer you some tea?"

"Please don't bother," Barbara said. "We just rose from lunch."

"No bother at all," Miss Giddens assured us, clutching at her voluminous nightgown, which looked about ready to fall off.

"Are you sure it's no bother?" Barbara asked, busy over a sketchy search of the room.

"Not at all. None whatever," said Miss Giddens amiably.

"Then we'll have some," said Barbara.

Miss Giddens was not embarrassed. She sat down in the rocking chair, nodded her head, and mumbled, "It's very kind of you—nothing so refreshing as a nice cup of tea. Milk and four lumps with mine, if you please."

It was clear that Uncle Alvin was not there, and Barbara and I turned to go. Miss Giddens was sorry to see us leave. "Come again soon," she said hospitably. "Next time, perhaps I can persuade you to have tea."

We thanked her and then went on downstairs where we made a thorough search, which included even the little balcony at the front and the cellar.

"He must be somewhere," Barbara said helplessly. "He couldn't disappear into thin air."

"He isn't down here, anyway. We'd better go upstairs again."

"I guess so," Barbara agreed with a worried frown. "He must be in one of the bedrooms, but how are we going to tell which one?"

We went back to the second floor and listened at the bedroom doors again. Apparently Mary and Grace were still sleeping quietly, but when we got to Papa's door we were startled to hear him talking.

"Dammit!" he was saying in a booming whisper, "I can't make her go to bed. As far back as I can remember she's never done as she was told. The only thing I can do is to tell her to stay up. That might work."

I opened the door and walked in, pulling Barbara with me. Papa was somewhat embarrassed because he was clothed only in a pair of pajamas that he had bought because I said they were terrible. They were not the sort of thing that even Papa would care to be seen in, and he made a hasty dive for his dressing robe.

It was not Uncle Alvin who was with him, but Dennis, neatly

robed and with a look of inquiry for us.

"When did you wake up?" I asked.

"I don't think I've been asleep."

"Oh yes, you have," said Barbara.

"I shouldn't want to contradict you, of course—but where did you get your information?"

"We heard you snoring," I put in impatiently.

"Impossible," said Dennis, "I never snore."

"Maybe you were pretending to snore?" Barbara suggested.

"No."

"All right—then you were snoring."

Papa guffawed, and Dennis said with dignity, "I may have drowsed for a moment, but something disturbed me, and then I heard you girls going downstairs."

"How did you know it was us ?" I asked.

"Aura of youth," Dennis said rather obscurely, "Anyway, I got up and looked over the banister and I saw you both come out of Miss Giddens' room and go downstairs. So I came down here to tell your father on you, but he admits that he has no control."

"No," I said, "but if you try Barbara's mother you'll get somewhere."

"Thanks," he said, "I believe I will. I must do something to get the house quiet so that I can sleep." He tightened the belt on his dressing robe, said good night to Papa, and made for the door.

"Take them with you, can't you?" Papa whined. "Don't you suppose I want some sleep too?"

"How?" asked Dennis.

"It's all right," said Barbara. "We'll go quietly."

"Good night," said Papa heartily and added under his breath, but grimly, "I'm going to lock and bolt the door."

We crept quietly up to the third floor but on the landing we ran into Mrs. Markham. She was practically wringing her hands.

"Where on earth have you been, Barbara? I've been nearly frantic and I don't know what to do. There's a strong smell of escaping gas up on the fourth floor."

CHAPTER EIGHTEEN

BARBARA BEGAN TO CRY. "It's Uncle Alvin," she said hysterically. "We must find him—they're killing him!"

"Uncle Alvin?" Mrs. Markham repeated helplessly.

"Oh, Mama, we must find him," Barbara sobbed. "He's disappeared—and we've looked everywhere.

Dennis was already on his way up the stairs. "I'll see if I can trace the smell of gas," he called back to us.

We all trailed up after him, sniffing loudly, but there was no smell of gas either on the stairs, or on the fourth-floor landing.

Barbara blew her nose and asked more composedly, "Are you sure it was gas you smelled, Mama?"

"Absolutely certain," said Mrs. Markham definitely. "I went to the bathroom and on my way back I realized at once that there was a strong odor of gas and it seemed to be coming from the stair well. I was going to rouse you, and then you all came up."

"Let's look in that vacant room, anyway," I suggested.

Dennis nodded and went in while we watched from the door—but there was no one in the room and no odor of gas. It was the same in Uncle Alvin's room, and when we laid our ears against the doors of the other two rooms we could hear nothing, nor was there any odor.

"There's something going on," Barbara whispered fretfully. "We must find him if it takes the rest of the night."

She told Mrs. Markham and Dennis about the missing drape and also about Miss Giddens' expected visitor, and they went at once to the windows on the stairs. Mrs. Markham shook her head, and her mouth tightened. "We shall have to phone the police at once. There may be some perfectly innocent explanation, but I cannot take the responsibility. And in the meantime we must make a determined effort to find Alvin."

Dennis nodded in agreement. "Suppose you go and telephone now, and the girls and I will start searching here on the fourth floor and work our way down. We'll stick together so that you need not be worried and we'll go into all the bedrooms to make sure."

"That's very sensible," Mrs. Markham agreed. "Thank you."

She went off downstairs, and Dennis decided that we would tackle Kate and Evie first. We roused them after banging on the door for a while, and Kate, sausaged into a purple flannel bathrobe, grudgingly permitted us to enter and look around. Evie sat up in bed and watched us with eyes like blue saucers.

"I don't see how I'm supposed to get up in the morning and attend to breakfast after being up all night," Kate grumbled, and added sharply, "You don't need to go tossin' them corsets around, Mr. Livingstone. I ain't got Mr. Mott hid under them."

"I don't see why your being up for five minutes during the night should interfere with breakfast," Barbara said crossly.

Kate folded her arms and stared at the doorknob. "You'd be surprised," she murmured.

"No, I wouldn't," said Barbara. "I know you and I know that breakfast will be either burned or underdone in the morning."

Dennis finished his search just then, and we withdrew, followed by an observation from Kate that we were chasing rainbows.

Neville, both interested and disturbed, was more polite. "It seems quite preposterous that anyone would want to hurt Alvin," he said fussily. "He must be around somewhere."

He was half inclined to come along with us and help us in our search but in the end he decided against it. He said he couldn't do his day's work faithfully if he did not get his proper sleep

We had only the bathroom after that, and since it proved to be quite blank and empty we went on down to the next floor.

We searched Barbara's room and mine again since we had been out of them for so long and then we went along to Camille's room.

Camille gave an agitated squeal when she saw Dennis and reached for a wrap trimmed with ostrich feathers. He promised to keep his eyes closed, and she fell back onto her pillow again. I could see that she was still quite drunk. We did not stay for long, and when we left she tried to follow us. Barbara turned back, pushed her onto the bed, and tucked the covers up around her chin. As far as I could see she dropped off to sleep before we had closed the door on her.

None of the rooms on the second floor had been divided, and there were only four. They were all large and represented Mrs. Markham's deluxe exhibits. They contained the best furniture and the boarders who had money.

Grace and Mary were both sympathetic about Uncle Alvin and willing that we should search their rooms, although Mary could not resist the observation that it was quite illegal. Dennis said it probably was and that he'd gladly go to jail if necessary.

Papa protested bitterly, but we searched his room just the same. He told us we were a bunch of old women, jumping to the conclusion that a man was murdered simply because he went out on a quiet binge.

This gave us a new idea, although we were careful not to let Papa see it. When we had finished his room we went straight down to the front hall to look at the hatrack.

However, Uncle Alvin's hat and coat were on their accustomed hook. Mrs. Markham was wringing her hands again and, after telling us that the police were en route, asked if we had searched everywhere.

Barbara said, "All but your room and Dennis'—and we're going right up now to do Miss Giddens'. We just came down to see if Uncle Alvin's coat and hat were still here."

"Did he have only one coat and hat?" I asked.

"Yes, yes, only one," said Mrs. Markham with an agitated glance at the limp coat and shabby hat on the rack. "But you must search every-where. Don't leave out any rooms. Go back now and do the ones you missed."

We turned to remount the stairs, and Dennis tried to stop us. "I'll go alone," he said. "You should stay with your mother, Barbara, and Diana should stay with you."

"Why?" I asked, following him up the stairs.

Barbara didn't bother to answer at all—she just came along.

We went right up to the third floor and poked around in Mrs. Markham's room. Barbara stuck her head out the window and viewed what was visible of the yard. "Nothing down there," she said briefly. "Not even Miss Giddens' shawl."

We went into Dennis' room, which was disorderly, without being messy, and bitterly cold. Barbara closed the window.

"What's the idea?" Dennis asked. "Is fresh air extra?"

"In the winter, in excess, yes," said Barbara. "Cost of heating."

We made for Miss Giddens' room after that, and on the way down-stairs I thought I detected a whiff of gas. I stopped, sniffing, and called to the others, but they could not smell anything, so we went on.

Miss Giddens was in bed with the covers over her head and only a tangled wisp of white hair showing. We switched on the light and poked around a bit, but apparently she did not wake up.

"She sleeps like a log," Barbara explained. "And complains of in-somnia all day."

We went to the stairs and found Mrs. Markham in the lower hall, staring up at us.

"We haven't found him," Barbara told her, descending. "And we've searched the entire house now."

"Then he is not here." Mrs. Markham turned away toward the

drawing room with her shoulders sagging a little.

She had turned on one light in the drawing room, and we all went in there and sat down to wait for the police.

Mary came down after a while, draped in a fancy negligee that I figured she had bought for her trousseau, if any. She sat down and lit a cigarette. "What's the matter? You haven't found him?"

Barbara said, "No," gloomily, and Dennis got up and began to move restlessly around the room. "I'm damned if I understand this," he muttered. "Where are those policemen?" He put an adjective in front of policemen, but I guess I was the only one who heard it.

Inspector Dodd and Schmaltz came in almost immediately after that and brought a couple of men with them.

"Where is it?" Schmaltz demanded loudly.

"Where is what?" Mary asked and chilled it all around with her most formidable schoolteacher manner.

Schmaltz wilted, and Inspector Dodd said courteously to Mrs. Markham, "You reported that Mr. Alvin Mott has disappeared?"

Mrs. Markham stood up. "He has been missing for some hours. We have searched the entire house, and yet his hat and coat are hanging in the hall and he has no others."

They examined the hat and coat and found only a soiled handkerchief in the pocket of the coat.

"You might look out in the yard," I suggested timidly. "The tulip bed has been dug up again, I believe."

Somewhat to my surprise, they trooped out into the yard without delay, leaving one of the men with us in the hall.

Neville came down while they were gone. "I can't sleep with all this going on," he explained staidly.

"But surely you cannot hear us on the top floor," Mrs. Markham protested.

"I can feel the undercurrents of unrest," said Neville sulkily.

The police came tramping back through the kitchen, and Schmaltz asked belligerently, "Who dug that bed up again?"

Barbara and I explained that Uncle Alvin had been intending to reset his bulbs, and then Mrs. Markham told them about the missing drape, and they went pounding up he stairs to look at the windows. Schmaltz said something about making a search of the house for themselves.

After they had gone we all went out to the kitchen and made some coffee. Neville had to be provided with a glass of milk, because he said he wouldn't sleep a wink if he touched coffee.

"Why do you want to sleep?" Mary asked. "With all this going on. You don't want to miss anything, do you?"

Neville begged her patiently not to lose her temper or her sense of proportion.

We drank our coffee and after a while we heard a fearful rumpus on the second floor and knew that Papa's room was being searched.

We went back to the drawing room and sat around for a while, and presently Neville got up restlessly and wandered into the hall. Almost immediately he let out a sharp cry, and we all started up and crowded out into the hall after him.

"My hat!" Neville squeaked furiously. "My overcoat! They're gone!"

CHAPTER NINETEEN

THE POLICE DEDUCED, with a great show of brilliance, that Uncle Alvin had gone off in Neville's hat and coat.

Neville was bitter about it. "They're too big for him," he kept saying. "If he had to filch an overcoat why couldn't he have taken something nearer to his size?" Which was absurd, because Dennis and Papa, the only other men in the house, were a good deal bigger than Neville.

Mrs. Markham made a valiant effort to defend her brother-in-law. "You know he's very absentminded, Neville. I'm sure that as soon as he discovers his mistake he'll bring your things back."

"He won't—he'll do no such thing," Neville snapped. "We all know he's gone off for a very good reason. Skipped. And even if he is apprehended I don't suppose I shall get my property back. I dare say it will be held as evidence."

"Evidence of what?" I asked and was drowned out by Schmaltz's booming voice.

Schmaltz said it was a good thing that Uncle Alvin had gone off in another guy's coat and hat, because it would make it easier to pick him up.

"I can't think where he could have gone," Mrs. Markham worried. "He knew nothing about hotels—I'm sure he could not have gone to one."

"Any dope can go to a hotel," Schmaltz said simply

Mrs. Markham set her mouth in an obstinate line and murmured, "Not Alvin."

We all went up to bed then, as instructed by Schmaltz. Mary left us on the second floor with the grim observation that it was a good thing tomorrow was Saturday, and Neville climbed up to the fourth floor, whining all the way about how he'd have to wear a sweater and cap that he kept for early-morning walks in Central Park. He said it was not appropriate for business and he did not know how the bank would take it.

"They'll fire you out on your ear," Barbara said and was promptly hushed up by her mother who told her to go to bed immediately.

"Yes, for God's sake, do," Dennis added. He gave Mrs. Markham a polite good night, threw a couple of careless ones at Barbara and me, and retired.

Mrs. Markham practically pushed us into our rooms and told us that if we did not stay put this time she'd inform Schmaltz on us.

It seemed to me, at that time, that I caught another whiff of gas, and I stood in the center of my room for a moment and sniffed violently—but the air was as pure as it ever gets in the back bedroom of a New York boardinghouse. I hesitated and then turned around and went out into the hall again.

Mrs. Markham had disappeared into her room, and the hall was empty, but I noticed the odor of gas—faint, yet quite distinct. I glanced up at the electric fixture on the wall beside me and saw that it was the same type as the one in my bedroom, with the electric bracket doing a graceful downward swoop and the gas jet curving away and upward.

The gas tap was slightly open, so that a small amount of gas was escaping, and I reached up and shut it off—and then stood there, wondering. I wondered why the thing had been turned on and who had done it. My first thought was that Evie might have brushed it accidentally while she was dusting, and then I decided sensibly that Evie would never waste time dusting the light fixtures. I reached up and ran a finger over the glass shade just to prove it, and the shade swung in and tinkled against the electric light bulb. My finger came away smudged with grime, and I ruled Evie out of the picture. Then who could have turned that tap? You could hardly kill anyone with a gas jet only half open out in the hall. I shrugged, gave it up, and went to bed.

I was almost asleep when a faint but clear tinkle brought me back to wide-eyed consciousness. It was a moment before I realized that someone had knocked the shade against the light bulb out in the hall, as I had done previously. I got out of bed and went quietly to my door with my heart thumping. I opened the door and cautiously stuck my head out—but there was nobody there at all. The hall stretched away, dim and vacant, and when I examined the light fixture I found it as I had left it, with the gas jet turned off.

I went back to bed and lay wide awake for some time, considering the thing. I came to the eventual conclusion that someone had deliberately turned the jet half on, and whoever it was had come back to turn it off. I turned over restlessly and realized that I had missed identifying this mysterious person by a very small fraction of time. I shivered under the warm bedclothes and wished myself anywhere but in Mrs. Markham's boardinghouse. I felt that I would have welcomed even the chance to go home with Papa.

I went off to sleep after a while but I was never very far below the surface, and at half-past eight I was awake again and so restless that I had to get up. I went in and took a hot bath and got down to the dining room a few minutes after nine.

Evie greeted me with exaggerated astonishment. "What in the world's come over you? I'll have to go and hurry Kate—she'd never have your breakfast ready at this time."

"Do so," I said, seating myself.

She returned with my breakfast in a comparatively short time, and I glanced around the empty room and asked, "Have they all eaten?"

Evie set her jaws into motion on a piece of gum that she kept hidden under her tongue when Mrs. Markham was about. "Yeah, they finished," she said. "Even that Schmaltz."

"How does Schmaltz get to eat with the gentry?"

"Most of the dames was here too," Evie said, surprised. "Schmaltz, he paid for his breakfast. Paid a quarter and gave me a nickel tip. I ast him what he expected me to do with it, and he told me to go and buy a new hat so he could take me out sometime."

"Wise guy," I said.

Evie nodded. "Sure—but he didn't get no change outa me. I told him the hat I bought in 1912 is good as new and maybe I better save the nickel for my income tax." She laughed heartily for a while and then went to work on her gum again.

"Any word of Uncle Alvin?" I asked.

"Nope. Disappeared into thin air, the way it looks. Wearin' old stick-in-the-mud's hat and coat, too—and did he look cute this morning! Sweater, cap, muffler, and gloves—and tears in his eyes."

"You'd think he'd have a second-best coat and hat," I said, laughing.

"Oh, that one!" Evie rolled her eyes. "He's a regular old woman about his clothes. I bet he folds his shorts away in lavender. He never keeps old clothes—when he's through with his things he gives them straight to the Salvation Army."

There was comparative silence for a moment while I drank coffee and Evie chewed gum.

"Evie, tell me," I said presently, "have you ever noticed that Uncle Alvin—Mr. Mott, to you—keeps a copy of *Elsie Dinsmore* in his room?"

"Sure."

"Do you know what *Elsie Dinsmore* is all about?"

"Well, I suppose it's about a girl called Elsie Dinsmore," she said indifferently.

"Clever."

"And don't think I don't know you meant that sarcastic."

"Will you listen?" I asked patiently. "That book is all about a little girl of eight. Do you think Mr. Mott would want to read a book about a little girl?"

"Not if I know him, he wouldn't."

"Well, where did he get the book, and when?"

"I don't know where," Evie said promptly, "but he got it about a couple months ago. I know because I thought I might loan it off him, but if it's kid stuff I guess I won't."

"Not a word in it that even a mothers' meeting could cavil at," I warned her as I stood up. "I guess I'll release you to your other duties now."

"Must you go?" she asked politely.

"I'm afraid so, but I've had a very pleasant time."

I went on through to the drawing room, where I found a glum-looking foursome. Mary and Grace were sitting on one couch, and Camille and Papa on another. Camille looked weak and washed out, but sober. She seemed to have given up sparkling at Papa.

He gave me an evil look as I walked in, and said, "You're getting ahead of yourself—far ahead. Actresses don't lie abed until they're made."

I raised my eyebrows. "Please, Papa! Keep your lewd jokes for the smoke room."

He blushed a fiery red, and I went on happily, "If you meant it innocently you shouldn't expose your provincial habit of getting up at six o'clock to the city slickers around here."

"You button up your flip tongue," he shouted, "or I'll wash your mouth out with soap. Good God! I'm jailed in here by a mob of reporters, with nothing to do but twiddle my thumbs—and I'm damned if I'm going to put up with your impertinence to boot."

I wandered over to the window and looked out, but there seemed to be no one around except a few men in a car parked at the curb. "There's no mob outside. Your own importance has gone to your head."

He stopped shouting and clothed himself in injured dignity. "I have already tried to go out," he said, pronouncing each word distinctly, "and I was besieged. So I came in again."

"What about Neville?" I asked. "Was he besieged too?"

Grace and Mary laughed. "What do you think?" Mary asked. "With that costume he was wearing."

I noticed, at that point, that Papa was quietly busy getting out cards and a bridge table. I knew that Camille did not play bridge and I tried at once to skip the room, and failed miserably. It was quite evident that Papa had been watching me out of the corner of his eye.

"No, you don't," he said, putting his solid bulk in front of me. "You owe me a few hours of bridge after what you did to me last night."

"I'm quite willing to take a hand, Papa," I said mildly. "But you can't very well force Grace and Mary to play."

"Nice try," Mary observed. "But no cigar. We've nothing else to do, so we might as well play bridge."

"But what about Camille?" I asked, knowing that it was no use. "I'm sure she doesn't want to watch. Seems rude."

"Camille," said Grace with finality, "must take the rough with the smooth."

I sighed and sat down with them, while Camille passed the remark, for Grace's benefit, that someone had once told her that only morons played bridge.

"That's quite correct," I said chattily. "We all know that Grace and Mary are morons, and I can vouch for Papa. I'm out of it, of course, since I play only when forced—"

"One spade," said Papa ominously.

The game droned on for a while, and then I asked, "Is there any news about Uncle Alvin?"

Mary shook her head. "Nothing. The Schmaltz man keeps saying it will be easy to pick him up because his hat and overcoat are too large for him, but how is Schmaltz to tell when a man's clothes don't fit him? His own coat won't button across his front, and it hangs down to just above his knees, while his hat covers both his eyebrows and his ears."

"You shouldn't be so critical," I said severely. "A man with a wife and four small children and girlfriends on the side must, of necessity, get his clothes from the Salvation Army."

"How do you know he has four small children?" Grace asked.

"He looks as if he had four small children," I said stubbornly. "In fact, I'm inclined to think it may be five."

Miss Giddens wandered in just then and, seeing a bridge game in progress, gamboled happily over and squashed herself in between Camille and me on the couch. Camille said, "Tch, tch," and stood up. Miss Giddens looked up at her and said, "Tch, tch, tch." Camille flounced off and brought a chair up and sat behind Papa.

I could not keep my mind on the game, and I could not keep it away from *Elsie Dinsmore*. It became such a thorn in my side, in fact, that I finally excused myself on a dummy hand and hurried all the way up the stairs to the fourth floor. I caught a glimpse of Barbara working in the bathroom, but she did not see me, and I went quietly into Uncle Alvin's room without disturbing her.

Elsie Dinsmore was still where I had last seen her, and I stepped over and picked the book up. It was *Elsie Dinsmore*, all right, but it was also Miss Opal's diary.

CHAPTER TWENTY

SQUARES OF WHITE PAPER, cut to fit, had been neatly pasted over the pages of the book, and on these Miss Opal had written her diary.

I clutched the book tightly in my hands and tiptoed to the door. Barbara was still working in the bathroom, whistling softly, and the hall was deserted, and after a hasty glance around I ducked out and hurried down to my room. Evie was there, languidly occupied in giving the floor a brief glimpse of a weary-looking mop, and the usual procedure was that when she had finished Barbara would be along to dust the furniture. But if I waited for Barbara Papa would most certainly start a manhunt from below and spoil everything. I hastily shoved the book into an empty suitcase, locked it, and hurried down the stairs.

Papa was already at the door of the drawing room prepared to start hue and cry. "Where in the name of God have you been?" he bellowed. "How the devil can we play bridge with you forever sneaking off? I'm going to get a doctor to you."

"Doctor?" I said, mystified, as I followed him into the drawing room.

"You must have weak kidneys, and they ought to be seen to."

"Heredity becomes both interesting and complicated," I said with dignity, "when a weakness in the parent's head comes out in the offspring's kidneys."

Miss Giddens and Camille were still there, and when I resumed my seat on the couch Miss Giddens shifted closer to me until her sharp little chin almost rested on my shoulder.

I was dummy again almost at once—since Papa's system was to play almost every hand himself. Sometimes it worked and sometimes it didn't.

I turned to Miss Giddens. "How are you feeling today?"

Miss Giddens said she hadn't had much sleep during the night.

"I'm sorry," I said politely. "What disturbed you?"

"I went for a walk."

"You went for a walk in the middle of the night?"

"Yes."

"Where did you go?" I asked.

But she had turned her attention to the cards and did not bother to answer.

I tried again. "Did you have a visitor last night?"

She glanced at me, nodded, and returned to the cards.

"Who was your visitor?"

She chewed on her false teeth and watched Papa trump an opposing ace with an ill-bred flourish.

I nudged her and asked, "Did you have a gentleman visitor?"

She nodded, "Charming man."

The hand ended, and I was pulled back into the game. I dealt, flipping the cards around the table and wondering despairingly how soon I could get away to read Miss Opal's diary. I was sure that once the police got their hands on it I'd never see it again and I felt that since I had found the thing alone and unaided I had a right to look it over first

To my dismay, the game dragged on until nearly lunch time. Twice I considered offering the excuse that I wasn't feeling well but I knew that Papa would immediately scare up at least two doctors and day and night nurses and I decided that it wasn't worth the fuss.

Grace saved me at last by saying that she had several papers to correct and she thought we'd better quit.

Mary said, "Oh, for heaven's sake, Grace! You have the whole weekend."

Grace's mouth became slightly schoolteacher. "I know, but they'll be on my mind until I get them done, and if we start another rubber now we'll probably run right into lunch, and over."

I sat with my fingers crossed while they argued it out and when Grace finally had her way I fled to my room. I hauled *Elsie Dinsmore* and Opal Rostrum out of the suitcase and sank comfortably onto my bed with a little sigh.

I had a minor interruption almost at once. Miss Giddens opened the door, walked in, and, with barely a glance at me, seated herself on the painted chair and proceeded to chew her cud.

I stared at her, and she turned her head and stared back. I wondered if there were any particular reason for her choosing my room to pass the time away and that probably she had simply followed me. Possibly, I reflected, she liked my smell, which was reasonable enough, because it cost me a pretty penny.

I turned my attention to the book and found that it covered a period of about two years. I had to wade through a lot of weather and comments on various books before anything interesting began to glimmer through. It came slowly, and Miss Rostrum hovered around, above and below the thing for several pages, before it was clear enough to be understandable. Boiled down to the essentials, it appeared that she and Uncle Alvin had fallen in love with each other and she had been afraid to let Imogene know. But apparently Imogene had suspected and was beginning to be restless and upset about it. Opal was all in a dither and seemed to be afraid that her sister would become violent if she learned the truth—so she had told Uncle Alvin that it could never be. Although just what it was that could never be was not quite clear. However, they might still meet secretly in the garden in summertime, for brief moments, and in the winter they would have to wait for spring.

Going on from there, it developed that Uncle Alvin was not satisfied with this and was pressing her. Actually, he wanted to marry her. Miss Opal's handwriting was all excited at this point.

From there on the diary was almost nothing but dramatic questions. Which is it to be? Sister or lover? The weather was noted only when it became really exceptional. Once she had written "I will keep this diary in Alvin's room from now on. Imogene does not suspect this innocent little book of *Elsie Dinsmore*—but she might happen to want to read it — although I know she read it several times when we were children. But she must not view what is written here, whereas Alvin may. I shall ask him to take it, and whenever I want it he will bring it to me."

"Very fine day," Miss Giddens commented.

I started and looked up. "No kidding," I said. "Is it really?"

"Yes, oh yes, indeed. Delightful."

I glanced at my watch. "It's lunch time, Miss Giddens."

She went like the wind, and since I had finished the diary I hauled myself off the bed, prettied up, and followed more slowly.

Papa was pacing the hall and fuming. "Where have you been now?" he barked. "You're almost half an hour late."

"Why didn't you go on in?"

"Because I have to be a ruddy gentleman," he snarled.

The dining room was one hundred percent occupied, with the single exception of poor Uncle Alvin. His small, individual table, close to the Rostrum's larger one, looked forlorn and lonely.

Mrs. Markham and Barbara looked tired, I thought. I knew there was extra work on Saturday, baking and things of that sort, and they had been up half the night as well.

Mary, Grace, and Dennis were quiet, almost subdued, and although Camille was offering them a line of talk they paid her very little attention. Neville was eating quietly, as became a gentleman, his eyes fixed absently on the bottle of pills that was a permanent fixture on his table. Miss Giddens was shoveling food into her mouth and pausing occasionally to retrieve stray bits that had fallen onto her bosom or the tablecloth.

Papa champed his way quickly through his portion and then told Evie to bring him a second helping of the main course. Evie's eyes popped, and her expression said plainly that in a boardinghouse you ate your allotted share and were satisfied.

I said, "Go and get him some more, Evie. You can make a note of it and put it on his bill."

"Well, I dunno," she said doubtfully. "I guess it's all right. The guys in that special room he has oughta be allowed extra food."

"You go and bring me what I ordered, my girl," Papa hissed, "and don't let me catch you discussing my diet with my daughter again, or I'll leave you the same kind of tip that you get from the rest of these people."

Evie departed at once and returned promptly with a heaping platter.

After lunch both Inspector Dodd and Schmaltz turned up, and we were put through an exhaustive questioning. They took over the dining room, and we were called in, sometimes singly, and occasionally in pairs. Barbara and I went in together and spent over an hour with them.

I handed over the diary at that time, and Dodd cursed Schmaltz out pretty freely for not having found it himself.

When they released us Barbara went upstairs to take a nap, and I returned to the drawing room, wondering what I was going to do with the afternoon and trying not to think of poor Uncle Alvin, wandering somewhere, alone and homeless.

Grace and Mary were taking their turn with Dodd and Schmaltz, and Papa was sitting by himself, playing solitaire. Mrs. Markham and Miss Giddens had disappeared, and Camille had ungracefully fallen asleep in her chair. Dennis was standing at the window, and when I seated myself he came over and sat beside me.

He said, "Tell me—you found Miss Imogene out on that little porch?"

"It's a balcony."

"All right, balcony. Now, was there any light on her? I mean, could anyone have seen her from the street?"

"No," I said, "it's dark in that corner. The bay window extends over the balcony, and the street light shines on the front-door side and throws a shadow at the other end."

"It's a bit involved," he said, "but I think I get you."

He walked over to the window again and took a look and then he came back. "Why would anyone put her out there?" he said thoughtfully.

"Well, you remember we were having supper in the kitchen that night."

He nodded. "And we heard a noise—which must have been someone pulling Miss Imogene downstairs. Whoever it was must have been badly frightened when he realized that someone was in the kitchen. I suppose he had intended dragging both the bodies through the kitchen and out into the yard, where the grave was already prepared."

"I guess that's the way it was," I said soberly. "But why bury them? Did he, or she, think they'd never be found?"

"I suppose so. Must have been some reason for going to all that trouble."

"But this person must have realized that the black portieres would be noticed," I said slowly. "I mean, that everyone would notice they had disappeared."

"That is an odd feature," he admitted. "You'd think a more inconspicuous shroud would have been selected. But I think it was done in a hurry—not planned for weeks in advance—or the portieres would never have been used. I think the Rostrums must have discovered something about Barbara, and Mott saw it too. What was she wearing?"

I thought it over for a moment. "She was dressed differently. I mean, she wore her blue when the Rostrums saw her and her black when Uncle Alvin dropped his coffee cup."

"Was there nothing she wore both times?" he asked.

"Well, she had that pin at her neck—Mary gave it to her for her birthday. It's a topaz, an old one, but it's good. Mary said she bought it in a little shop downtown."

He shook his head and was silent for a moment. "I don't see that that helps much," he said presently. He glanced at the window. "I still don't see why Miss Imogene was lugged out onto that balcony. It was dangerous, because she must have been highlighted when she was carried out the front door—if, as you say, the street light shines in there."

I looked up at the windows and studied them for a moment before replying. They were old-fashioned—large and nearly reaching to the floor, although they were not French doors, but the usual sash type. Dennis followed my eyes, and I said, "She wasn't taken out the door. She was put through the window."

"I believe you're right." He went over and raised one of the windows, and it slid up easily and without noise. He closed it again and came back. "Our murderer was in a bit of a tight corner," he said, speaking as much to himself as to me. "He brought Miss Imogene down, expecting the lower floor to be deserted, and then he heard us in the kitchen—and must have heard us stand up and knew that we were coming out into the hall. He must have worked quickly—pushed up the window and shoved the body out. The portiere came off, and he simply folded it and put it up on top of the sideboard. He'd have had to duck into the dining room from the drawing room when we came into the hall. Barbara came then, and we all went to bed. Which left the coast clear, and yet the murderer must have gone to bed, too, without completing the job. Why?"

"It's curious," I admitted, "because Miss Opal was still in Miss Giddens' room and Miss Giddens was getting restless about it."

Papa boomed out suddenly, from across the room, "Livingstone! Kindly keep away from my daughter."

Dennis glanced idly at Camille, who was snoring slightly, with her mouth hanging open. "Not until you keep away from my Camille."

I heard Barbara's quick step on the stairs, and she came into the room. She gave a quick look around, caught sight of me, and came up and put her lips against my ear.

"That missing drape," she whispered, "is in one of your bureau drawers."

CHAPTER TWENTY-ONE

I JUMPED UP IN A HURRY, and Dennis asked, "What is it? What's the matter?"

"Nothing," I said hastily. "Nothing at all. It's just that Barbara wants me to do something for her."

I caught Barbara's arm and urged her out of the room. "Who put it there?" I whispered as we went up the stairs.

"Search me," she said, shrugging. "It's in your underclothing drawer and it's such a tight squeeze that you can hardly get the drawer open. I washed those stockings I borrowed from you and I went to the drawer to put them back. I had to pull and jerk around before I could get it open and then I found that drape stuffed in there."

We reached my room, and the drape was still in the drawer, which Barbara had left half open. The cloth was a wine-colored velour, and I pulled it out of the drawer and held it up. "Are you sure it belongs to that window on the stairs?"

"Of course I'm sure," Barbara said. "The other one is just the same. But how did it get in here?"

"How should I know? Somebody's trying to frame me, I guess."

"Oh well," said Barbara philosophically, "you needn't worry about that. Your father's so rich, he'll be able to get you off, no matter what they arrest you for."

"That's very comforting," I said with a touch of bitterness, "but I'd prefer not to be arrested at all. I'm going to plant this thing somewhere else, unless you feel bound to tell them you found it here, in which case I'd rather go down and tell them myself, first."

She said, "Don't be silly. Of course I'm not going to tell them. They're paid to find things out for themselves."

I shook my head. "Barbara, your economic sense is a trifle distorted. But passing that over for the moment—where shall I put this drape? Because it's not going to stay here."

"What are you talking about?" Barbara said indignantly. "I had economics in school, and in this case—"

"Be quiet! We have to decide where to put this thing, so that I can save my own skin. I don't want to get anyone else into trouble either."

Barbara wrinkled her forehead for a moment, and then her face cleared. "Miss Giddens' room. It can't possibly do her any harm, since they already found bodies and things in there."

I nodded on a breath of relief and, folding the drape as tightly as possible, I tucked it under my arm. We went quietly and cautiously out into the hall and came face to face with Inspector Dodd and Schmaltz, who had just come quietly—and perhaps cautiously, too—up the stairs.

I kept the drape pinned under my arm but I had a distinct sensation that it was burning me.

Dodd stepped courteously to one side to allow us free passage. "You girls go on downstairs. We're going to be busy on this floor."

We crept down the stairs through a fog of guilt and expecting every minute to be called back and asked for an explanation as to why I had the missing drape under my arm.

Nothing happened, however, and we made Miss Giddens' room in safety. We stuffed the drape onto the floor of her closet on top of a lot of other junk and then collapsed onto a couple of chairs, wiping our brows.

"Wow!" said Barbara.

"Don't be vulgar. Actresses don't use slang expressions."

"I think you're wrong about that," said Barbara. "However, 'Oh deah!' if you like that better."

I noticed, just then, that Miss Giddens was in residence. She had her head stuck out the back window and as I watched she drew it in, closed the window, and turned around. She looked at us without any special interest and observed, "I've dropped it out of the window."

"That's too bad," said Barbara, "What did you drop? Your teeth?"

"No, no," said Miss Giddens impatiently, "not my teeth. See, I have my teeth." She took them out and waved them in front of us.

I muttered, "Oh God!" and closed my eyes.

Barbara said hastily, "Put them back in again quickly, because I want to give you some candy."

Miss Giddens promptly restored her dentures, and Barbara fished a piece of chewing gum from her pocket.

"She might swallow it," I said doubtfully.

Barbara shrugged. "So what if she does? She ate a box of colored crayons once, under the impression that they were candy. Nothing will ever kill her."

Miss Giddens informed us again, and rather more pointedly, that she had dropped something out of the window.

"Was it your shawl?" Barbara asked.

"No, no, no, not my shawl. Certainly not."

"She's right, for once," I said, gesturing toward the bureau where the shawl was hanging half over the mirror.

"Let's have a look and see what it is then."

"Wait a minute—suppose we test her," I suggested. "See if she gets anything right. And then we'll look and check up."

"Okay." She turned to Miss Giddens and asked slowly and clearly, "What did you drop out of the window?"

Miss Giddens blinked, nodded, and said, "Yes."

"Shall I go and get it for you?" Barbara asked.

"Yes, please—you get it for me. Very kind of you."

"What shall I get for you?" Barbara persevered. "Is it your shawl?"

"My shawl, yes," said Miss Giddens gratefully. "I think I should put it on—it's a little chilly. But I dropped the key out of the window, you know."

We both made a dive for the window and flung it open. We stuck our heads out and found that Miss Giddens' head was right in amongst us.

We could not see anything, though, so we closed the window and decided to go down and investigate. As we left the room Miss Giddens opened the closet door and said, "Good afternoon," into the closet.

We went through the lower hall and the deserted dining room to the kitchen, where we found Kate making the Saturday-night apple pies.

"Where are you going?" she asked, resting her hands on her hips.

"Out into the yard to play," said Barbara.

"You betta not," Kate warned ominously. "Them cops will pick up your footprints and arrest you. They nearly arrested me already. Says I took some curtain down to wash and lost it instead. I told them any time they seen me doing laundry work around here they better go get their eyes looked at, and what's more, I never lost anything in my life."

"That's telling them," said Barbara, moving toward the door.

Kate shifted a hairpin, sniped, and picked up the rolling pin. "They're turnin' the house upside down now, lookin' for this same curtain."

I slid out the door after Barbara, and we exchanged a faintly guilty glance. "Anyway," said Barbara defiantly, "we gave them their chance. We walked right in front of their noses with the thing, and they wouldn't look. I guess they're just shiftless."

We walked over to a spot directly beneath Miss Giddens' window and after a brief search we found the key. It was a large, old-fashioned iron thing, and Barbara identified it as one of the bedroom-door keys. I knew that very few of the boarders bothered to lock their doors, and Barbara pointed out that that type of key usually opened several locks beside its own.

I took a look at the tulip bed before we went in. It was still dug up, with bulbs lying around here and there. I shivered and wished, somehow, that they would leave it alone.

We went back to the second floor and before we entered Miss Giddens' room we tried the key in the lock of the door. It went in easily enough, but at the same time we heard a key fall to the floor on the other side. We went in and, ignoring Miss Giddens, who looked rather startled, we picked the key from the floor and put it back into the lock. It locked the door, all right, and evidently belonged there.

We showed Miss Giddens the key we had found in the yard and asked her where it belonged. She looked at it for a moment and then took it into her hand and immediately made for the window. We rushed her and got it away from her and then considered the situation for ourselves.

There were three doors in the room—the one that opened into the hall, the closet door, and one that connected the room with Mary's. We tried the closet door first and found that the key fitted perfectly.

"That's it then," Barbara said rather flatly.

"Let's try the connecting door anyway," I suggested, and she nodded.

The key fitted the door leading to Mary's room quite as well, and, to our surprise, we found that it was already unlocked.

"Mary will have a fit," Barbara said. "Imagine Miss Giddens being free to roam through your room at will."

"Well, but Mary never locks her door anyway. Anyone in the house could roam through her room."

"Having a connecting door makes it much easier, though. This key belongs on Mary's side of the door—it's always been there. I'll bet Miss Giddens got into her room, unlocked this door, and walked into her own room, taking the key with her."

"Or else she didn't."

"All right, or else she didn't. Let's go."

We went through into Mary's room, locked the connecting door after us, and left the key in the lock.

Out in the hall we were joined by Miss Giddens, wearing her hat and coat, and we all went downstairs together.

In the drawing room Mary, Grace, Dennis, and Papa were playing bridge in a women-against-the-men arrangement. Camille was hovering on the outskirts, and Neville was sitting in a far corner reading a newspaper in a rather austere manner.

Barbara and I sat down, prepared to mingle sociably, and within ten minutes of our arrival the room was empty, save for Miss Giddens, still adorned with hat and coat, and ourselves.

"You'd think we had the plague," Barbara said and I added, with a glance at Miss Giddens, "Maybe it's the company we keep."

Papa was the first one to come back. He appeared with a large, expensive-looking box of candy, and I asked curiously, "For whom?"

"For me," he said with a touch of defiance. "I'm very fond of chocolates, and all my life I've had to buy them for women and then felt like a hog for taking too many when they were offered to me."

He foolishly laid the box down on the bridge table for a moment, and before he could turn around Miss Giddens was quietly carrying it to a chair in the bay window. She began to eat the chocolates with astonishing speed and spent the time between bites in pawing over those remaining in the box.

I laughed, but Barbara frowned and made an effort to get them away from her.

"Don't bother, little girl," Papa said hastily. "I—er—don't believe I'd care to eat them now." He glanced at his watch and added irritably, "Where the devil are those people?"

"You mean they're coming back?" I asked.

"Damn right, they're coming back. Catch them quitting now—they're all winning from me."

"You overbidding again?"

"I never overbid," said Papa coldly.

Mary came in and said, "Oh, Barbara, I wonder if you could dig up a key for my room. With all this that's been going on, I think I should lock my room at night."

"Maybe the key in that door to Miss Giddens' room would fit your hall door," Barbara suggested.

"Yes, it does, I know," Mary said, "but, you see, it has disappeared. I have just looked for it."

CHAPTER TWENTY-TWO

BARBARA'S EYES STRAYED to mine, and she assumed an air of casual interest. "I wonder what could have happened to it? But, anyway, don't worry. I'll dig up another one for you."

She got up and made for the hall, and I followed close at her heels. When we reached the second floor we met Grace, who was coming out of her room, and Barbara hailed her. "Mary says the key to that connecting door in her room is missing. Did you take it, by any chance?"

"Not by any chance," said Grace. "Anything that passes between us goes from me to Mary."

We waited until she had disappeared down the stairs and then we slipped into Mary's room. The key was missing, all right, nor could we find it on the floor, and the door was still locked.

We went around into Miss Giddens' room, but there was only the key in her hall door, and we could not find another. "I'll try this one in Mary's door," Barbara said. "I don't think Miss Giddens should have one anyway."

But Miss Giddens' key would not fit either Mary's hall door or the connecting door, and Barbara swore softly. "Let's go and look out of Miss Giddens' window," she said in exasperation. "Maybe she threw it out again."

"Don't be silly. She's been treading on our heels ever since we left the key in the connecting door and went downstairs. Someone else took it away, and the question is, why?"

"Well, of course," Barbara said slowly, "most of them didn't bother with keys before, and now they're all starting to want one. Someone might have pinched it simply to use in his own door."

I shook my head. "I don't think so."

"I don't, either," said Barbara, "but we can't prove anything one way or the other. Let's go."

We went on downstairs and ran into Schmaltz in the front hall.

Barbara hesitated and then spoke up. "Mr. Schmaltz, there's a key missing."

Schmaltz said, "No kiddin', girlie. Shall I ring up the commissioner and have all the boys sent around to find it for you?"

"Not at all," said Barbara, looking offended. "I wouldn't have the boys take their feet off their desks for the world. I'll just have the door taken away."

She flounced into the drawing room, and I followed, while Schmaltz looked after her and fished a toothpick from his vest pocket.

Camille and Neville were still absent, but the bridge game had started up again, and Miss Giddens was still in her chair in the bay window. The box of chocolates was in her lap, but she had stopped eating them and was looking a bit sick.

Barbara glanced at her and said, "It's a shame—the poor thing has eaten too many. Your father should never have given them to her."

Papa looked up from his cards and bleated unhappily, "Good God, girl, you saw her snatch them from me. What was I supposed to do?"

Mary and Grace began to laugh, and Mary observed, "You ought to watch your weight a little anyway, Mr. Prescott. Good thing she took them from you."

Papa cast an involuntary glance down over his facade. "Miss Mary," he said with rather startling mildness, "my weight has only recently been approved by my doctor."

I stared at him for a moment and then I said, "Lay off, Papa. Mary wants love rather than riches."

"Hold your tongue!" he roared.

Dennis, who was still partnering Papa, had the couch seat, and Barbara and I sat down on each side of him. We draped ourselves more or less on his shoulders to see what effect it would have on Grace and Mary, but they both kept stiff upper lips.

Mary presently ran a well-shaped hand through her thick, curling hair and said thoughtfully, "I don't know—sometimes I think that riches would be more satisfying than love, at that." Which I took to be a threat.

I called her bluff promptly. "You can have Papa if you'll guarantee me an allowance—"

"Five dollars a week is more than ample for a child of your age," she said equably, "and you'll get not a penny more." She leaned across and tapped Grace on the arm. "I'll not be stepping on your toes, dear, if I pick up this gent?"

"Not at all," said Grace politely.

"Godammit!" growled Papa, beginning to lose his temper. "Can't I get simple respect from anybody?"

"Go to the phone," I suggested, "and order a fur coat for each of them, and they'll sew a piece of red carpet under your shoes."

Papa bellowed, "Two spades!" and Mary's double was prompt and emphatic.

Dennis quivered from head to foot with rage, and when he was able to speak he said coldly, "I'll marry your daughter for that, Prescott."

"Just tell me when," said Papa, "and I'll be at the church with a gun. Anyway, you don't know what I have in my hand."

"I can guess," Dennis said bitterly.

"Leave my name out of your barroom brawls," I interposed acidly.

Dennis caught my chin, tilted my face, and kissed me. "It's all right, honey. No disrespect intended."

Papa said furiously, "Diana! Get away from that man."

"Leave her alone," said Grace tolerantly, "she's having fun."

"Is this a goddam bridge game, or are we playing post office?" Papa yelled.

Dennis dropped his cards onto the table and said agreeably, "Post office suits me."

"Well, it doesn't suit me," said Mary briskly. "I'm working toward my new winter coat—and it's two spades, doubled. Diana, you and Barbara run along and see about getting me that key."

Barbara and I were out in the hall before we realized that Mary's schoolteacher talent had sent us there and that we hadn't really wanted to go. We nearly went back then but were stopped by what sounded like Papa proposing to Mary.

"I mean it," he was saying earnestly. "Young and attractive as you are, and able to control my daughter like that! You can name the day—and you can run right down and buy a trousseau on me."

"Stop!" said Mary. "I'm getting dizzy and I think I'm weakening."

Barbara pulled me back into the hall. "We can't go in now—it isn't ethical. In case Mary wants to marry your father we mustn't spoil the illusion he has that she can control you."

I sat down on the stairs and said, "But wait a minute. I'm not sure I want Mary to marry him."

Barbara looked slightly shocked. "Don't be such a pig. As if there wasn't enough for both of you!"

"I'm not thinking about that," I said hastily. "I just meant that I don't know whether Mary could make him happy."

"Well, what about Mary's happiness?" said Barbara indignantly.

I sighed. "Let's quit, because we're not getting anywhere. Papa is a cad, and I'm a pig because we don't snatch Mary into the bosom of our family. Are you forgetting Grace? Maybe he should marry her as well."

"You're talking like an infant," said Barbara. "Mary would bring color into your father's life."

"Listen, if Papa gets any more color in his life he'll go blind for sure."

"Well," she said, shrugging, "I don't mind telling you I'm all for the engagement."

Schmaltz, emerging from the dining room, heard her and asked, "Who's engaged?"

We stared at him in silence.

"Come on, girls, spill it. Who's engaged?"

I drew a long breath and said, "It's supposed to be a secret, but I'm sure I can trust you to treat it confidentially. It's Neville and—and Miss Giddens."

Schmaltz said, "Now, girlie, don't get funny. That guy would make a good hole for any doughnut, but I guess he's got his limits."

"Did you ever hear of money?" I asked, narrowing my eyes at him.

Schmaltz whistled and said simply, "Why, the lousy bum!"

Miss Giddens padded out into the hall with her hat hanging on one side of her head.

"Did you have a nice walk?" Barbara asked.

"Very nice, indeed," said Miss Giddens amiably. "Delightful. Only I didn't go out. Bad weather, you know."

She started up the stairs, and Schmaltz put a courteous hand under her elbow. "Congratulations on your engagement," he said loudly.

"Thank you," said Miss Giddens.

"Where is he?" Schmaltz asked, raising his voice another notch with the evident idea that the louder he spoke, the better chance he had of reaching her brain. "I want to congratulate him too."

"He is up in my bedroom now," said Miss Giddens. "I am just going up to him."

"Well, for Chrissake!" said Schmaltz, staring after her.

"Come on," Barbara said to me. "I want to go down to the cellar and dig up some keys."

We went on through the kitchen, which was humming with activity attendant on preparations for the evening meal. Kate and Evie were rushing wildly to and fro like a couple of madwomen.

The cellar was fairly small, since the house was tall rather than wide, and it was dim and gloomy. Barbara found a bunch of keys in an old, mildewed bureau, and we turned to go upstairs.

We both stopped at the same time.

"Something burning," I said, sniffing.

Barbara nodded. "That's what I thought."

We poked around uneasily but we could not find anything burning except the furnace. Barbara pulled the iron door open, at last, to see if there was anything in there besides coal.

There was. We could see the charred pages and general outline of a book, and there were some fragments of cardboard which might have been photographs. Close to the door, where the fire was not so hot, lay the topaz pin which Mary had given to Barbara.

CHAPTER TWENTY-THREE

BARBARA CRIED, "Oh, my pin!" and looked frantically around for something with which to lift it out.

"It's no use," I said, staring at the glowing coals. "The thing's ruined."

She slammed shut the creaking iron door and said furiously, "I'm going to tell the police. It's a rotten shame when they're lounging all over the house, and still a person's property isn't safe."

"We'd better hurry," I agreed. "Schmaltz ought to have a look at that stud before it's completely destroyed."

We went upstairs and passed through the kitchen where Kate was urging Evie, in a raucous voice, to knock her head against the iron stove and see which cracked first. Evie was whistling unconcernedly.

We found Schmaltz in the front hall, shrugging himself into his overcoat.

"Take it off," said Barbara. "There's something in the cellar you ought to see."

Schmaltz took it off, flung it onto the floor, and pounded out to the kitchen in a fury. Barbara and I followed, but by the time we got there he had already disappeared into the cellar.

Kate said, "How-do. Nice to see you after all this long time. I like it fine when you play hide-and-seek in my kitchen just before dinner—I don't get so lonesome."

"Shut up, Kate," said Barbara briefly, and we went on down the cellar stairs, where we found Schmaltz standing at the foot, making a brave effort to keep a civil tongue in his head.

"Did you look?" Barbara asked.

"Did I look where, and for what?" said Schmaltz, quivering.

"Why, in the furnace, of course. My best pin and a book and some other stuff."

Schmaltz made for the furnace, flung the door open, and took a quick look inside. He left the door hanging open while he raced around the cellar until he found an old pair of tongs. He fished the brooch out, but it appeared to be ruined, the stone blackened and dull and the setting twisted and melted out of recognition. The book fell to pieces as the tongs touched it, and the pieces of cardboard had disappeared, save for a corner of one of them that had fallen onto the unburned coal at the side.

Schmaltz gingerly worked it out and then stood for a while, holding it in his hand and staring at it thoughtfully.

"Old-type post-card-size photograph," he said presently.

"How can you tell?" Barbara asked, impressed. "I think that's pretty clever."

Schmaltz expanded a little and said in an offhand manner, "That's easy. We gotta drawer full of these things at home. All the old woman's ugly-puss relations." He loosed a guffaw that brought Evie to the head of the cellar stairs.

"This is one of the same," he went on, "and we got to find out whose it is." He looked at us as though he thought we might be able to tell him.

"I don't see how you'll ever find that out," Barbara said dubiously. "The house must be full of old photographs. I guess Mother has some, and Uncle Alvin. And I'll bet the Rostrums had them piled up in stacks."

"Sure," said Schmaltz, "we've got all those." He fingered the ruined brooch and asked, "Now, what's this piece of jewelry?"

Barbara identified it and then had to spend nearly ten minutes explaining that although the pin was hers she had not thrown it into the furnace herself.

Schmaltz still had an open mind on the subject when he left us. He said that if we happened to track down a missing photograph or book he'd appreciate it if we'd let him know.

After he had gone we went upstairs to wash up a bit for dinner.

"Are there many books around the house?" I asked.

"No," Barbara said, "I think we have more chance of tracing the book than the photograph. My father had quite a library, but Mama sold it in one lot after he died. I'll go through the few we have and see if I can find one missing, and I want to look over our old photographs too."

I had brought five books with me, and they were all still in my room, and I had no photographs.

I tidied myself in a bit of a hurry and found that I was inclined to glance uneasily over my shoulder from time to time. The house had become a creeping horror to me, and I felt a sudden hysterical determination to leave.

The dinner gong sounded as I went downstairs, but I found the drawing room deserted, so I went back up to the second floor. Papa was not in his room, so I looked in Mary's room, where I found him with Mary, Grace, Neville, and Miss Giddens.

They had drinks but they looked bored stiff and they barely troubled to notice me.

"What's the matter?" I asked. "Why the gloom?"

"Is there any particular reason for us to be gay?" Mary asked acidly. "Your father lost at bridge, and Dennis blamed him, and they quarreled."

"What do you mean?" I asked. "They're not even speaking."

"They were," said Mary significantly.

"So where's Dennis?"

Mary shrugged, and Papa said, "Sulking. What's it to you, anyway?"

"Papa, listen," I said suddenly. "Let's get out of here."

"Smell something you don't like?" Mary asked, bristling up.

"I don't mean your room," I explained. "It's the whole house. I—I'm scared. Let's go home for a while, Papa, right now—before tonight. Somehow, I don't like tonight."

"It might be the gladdest, merriest night of the whole year," Mary put in grimly. "And you'd miss it."

Papa heaved himself to his feet. "It's not a bad idea," he said. "I'd like to get out of the place, myself—nothing I'd like better. I'll have to speak to Dodd though. I promised him that I would before I left."

"It's dinner time," Neville announced primly and went out, followed closely by Miss Giddens.

"I guess we can eat something first," I said, "but let's leave right after dinner."

Papa nodded. "All right, I'll do what I can. But I might have a little difficulty."

"No, you won't. A big canner like you wouldn't have any trouble."

Papa strutted a little. "Well, well—perhaps," he murmured modestly.

"After the revolution," Grace observed, "wealthy people will no longer have more influence than poor people."

"Commissar Prescott will personally see to it," I agreed.

As we left the room Mary said wistfully, "It's a shame that Dennis isn't Papa Prescott and that I'm not married to such a combination of wealth and beauty."

Camille was sitting in the drawing room, smoking a cigarette. She mashed it out when she saw us and asked brightly, "Going in to dinner?"

I smiled and nodded, but Papa took no notice because his mind was elsewhere. Camille attached herself to us, and we went into the dining room together. I reflected idly that Camille never made a solitary entrance into the dining room; she always waited for someone, even if it had, of necessity, to be Miss Giddens.

Everyone was present, but they were unusually quiet, and even Evie found nothing to say. Gloom lay over the place like a fog, and I found myself yearning toward our hideous upstate mansion—that Papa had designed himself. A picture of it kept floating into my mind, and instead of shuddering, as usual, I felt an aching desire to be there.

Miss Giddens finished first, as she usually did, and padded out of the dining room, sucking reminiscently at her teeth. She returned again almost immediately and asked for some cake to take up to her room. Evie gave her some odd bits, and she trotted off.

We dribbled into the drawing room after dinner, and Barbara drew me to one side. "There are no books missing," she whispered. "Mama and I went through them, and we're both pretty sure they're all there. We're going to do the photographs now."

Dodd appeared after a while, and Papa promptly buttonholed him. They talked in low voices for a while, and then Dodd slipped out, and Papa came over to me. "Seems it would be better all around if we stayed for a while. I gather that you're more or less of a material witness, and this fella, Dodd, would appreciate it if we remained. Now, I always believe in upholding the law and supporting the police, so I told him we would."

"Did you tell him how you upheld the police that time you got a ticket for going through a red light?" I asked bitterly.

Before he could tell me, for the three-hundred-and-seventh time, that it had been an orange light, Neville tapped him on the arm and asked him if he'd care to make a fourth at bridge.

He forgot me at once and said, "Certainly, certainly— very glad to. Who else will play?"

I edged around behind a chair with my fingers crossed, but Neville said, "I believe Miss Mary and Miss Grace would like a game."

"Delighted," said Papa genially. "You collect the Misses Grace and Mary and the table and cards. I'll gladly make a fourth."

Neville rushed off to do Papa's bidding, and I slipped out into the hall. I stood there uncertainly for a moment and then I decided to go up to my room and see if the key to my door was still in its lock.

The third floor seemed to be deserted, and the hall was only dimly lighted. I hurried into my room, shivering, and was almost surprised to see that the key was still in the door. I stood looking at it for a while and I remembered Barbara saying that the keys to the bedroom doors were often interchangeable, and we had subsequently proved it to ourselves.

I drew a slightly unsteady breath and made up my mind to have a bolt on my door. I felt sure that Barbara could find one for me and I was determined to have it on the door before I went to bed.

I stepped out into the hall—and my heart seemed to stop altogether. Something was standing near the head of the stairs, and it was muffled from head to foot in the wine-colored drape.

CHAPTER TWENTY-FOUR

I HAD A WILD, nightmare sort of idea that the corpse intended for that drape was now in it, and I lost my head completely. I screamed shrilly and dived back into my room. I ran right over to the window and crouched down onto the floor with my face hidden. I heard my door open but I did not dare to look around. I screamed again and had a confused hope that I would faint before the thing could get to me.

I did not faint, and nothing happened until several people poured into my room at once. I turned my head fearfully and saw that Inspector Dodd was foremost in the ranks. "What is it? Quick!" he snapped.

I quavered, "Oh, hurry!" And then my voice gave out.

Mrs. Markham came forward, and, with her firm little hands on my elbows, raised me to my feet. "Come, now, Diana, you must tell us what frightened you. It's important for the police to know quickly."

I took a long breath and told them, and they all surged out into the hall again, leaving me to die there alone. I gave my head a shake, swallowed a couple of times, and followed them.

The rest of the house had congregated out in the hall, up to and including Miss Giddens. She asked me what they were all doing, and I told her they were chasing rainbows.

Dodd had none of his assistants with him, and he sent Evie downstairs to call one of them in. I had a blurred idea that he told her she'd find one parked in a car in front of the house.

In the meantime Kate had discovered the drape. It was hanging on the newel post of the stairs leading to the fourth floor and had been draped completely over the post with the folds at the bottom spread out in a semicircle on the floor.

Dodd shrugged and said flatly, "That's what you must have seen, of course."

"It wasn't—I didn't," I stammered. "Look." I walked over to the head of the stairs leading from the second floor. "It was standing right here. Besides, it—the drape wasn't arranged the way it is now."

Papa, who had been patting my back, said, "Never mind, baby, what you need is a good night's sleep."

"You don't believe me!" I declared angrily.

"Of course I do," Papa protested. "Certainly." But I could see that he didn't, and neither did the others. They offered me bits of stilted sympathy and departed, one by one. I thought helplessly that they did not want to believe me anyway. They would not want to cope with the idea that a corpse was walking around the house wrapped up in a curtain.

I shuddered, and Papa gave me several more pats and said, "There, there."

Dennis was still with us, and he asked, "Did you notice whether it was wearing shoes?"

I shook my head, feeling foolishly inadequate. I had seen nothing but the drape.

"Of course it didn't have shoes," said Papa heartily. "You come on down to the drawing room for a while, petty, where it's light and cheerful."

"And watch you play bridge?"

"We haven't started to play yet," he explained. "Due to start at nine-thirty. The others had various little duties to perform in their own rooms first, so I went up to mine. I was cheating at solitaire when I heard you yell."

"Where was it standing?" Dennis asked, coming to the surface after a lot of deep thought.

I pointed to the spot as Papa whisked me past him and down the stairs.

Dodd was busily engaged in arranging a quiz party to find out where the drape had been between their search for it and its arrival on the newel post. Barbara and I could have given him a hint, of course, but I caught her eye upon me and decided to fall in with her idea of saying nothing. Dodd got quite irritated when he found that no one could give him the right answers, and he finally stamped out to the kitchen, presumably to heckle Kate and Evie.

As soon as he had gone I tackled Barbara about a bolt for my bedroom door, but she seemed a bit dubious. "They're all asking for keys and things, and I'm having quite a time trying to keep up with the demand. The next one that asks me, I'm going to tell them to file an application and it will be given a hearing in due order."

Mrs. Markham said, "Now, Barbara. You shall have some sort of a secure lock for your door, Diana, so don't let it trouble you."

"Did you find any books or photographs missing?" I asked her.

"I'm sure the books are there, but I have not had an opportunity to go through the photographs yet. I believe I'll do it now."

"We'll come and help," Barbara decided. "Come on, Diana."

I glanced at Papa, but he was preparing for his bridge game and seemed to have forgotten me, so I went along with the Markhams.

When we arrived on the third floor I began to wish that I had stayed in the drawing room. I knew, even if no one else did, that someone had stood in the hall, wrapped in that drape, and insanity seemed the only way to account for it. But they all seemed normal enough except Miss Giddens, and she was physically frail and appeared to be quite harmless. I supposed it was possible that some stranger had broken in, although the police had searched the entire house. And yet they had searched for the drapes too, and had not found it even when they saw it tucked under my arm. Only you could not tuck a burglar under your arm, nor stuff him into a bureau drawer.

We went into Mrs. Markham's room, and she walked to her desk and pulled open a drawer. "I believe most of the photographs are here."

She took them out in neat little piles and put them on the bed. There were all kinds—men with fancy mustaches and women with pompadours and bows.

"These old-fashioned pictures are the important ones," Mrs. Markham said thoughtfully. "That man Schmaltz seems to think it was this type that was burned. I'll go through these, and you girls can look over all the snapshots. We'd better hurry a little because Schmaltz said that he would be back shortly after nine, and he wants to know about it."

There were two studio portraits of Barbara which I admired for a while, and then she and I started in on the snapshots. We found them quite interesting and often hilarious. There were dozens of Barbara and a fair amount of Mrs. Markham and Uncle Alvin. There was one of Uncle Alvin's wife—Mrs. Markham's sister—who had died in childbirth.

Mrs. Markham glanced at it and heaved a conventional sigh. "Poor Alvin," she said, "he never got over losing Nan."

She dropped a picture, that she had been holding, of a portly gentleman half hidden behind a growth of beard and twisted her hands together. "I wish we could find him, or at least hear that he's well and happy. I can't understand it—how he could be mixed up in this terrible affair."

"Now, don't you get yourself all upset, Mama," Barbara said. "Finish up with your photographs. There's no use in your worrying about Uncle Alvin. You can't do anything, and he's probably all right anyway."

"I wish I could think so," Mrs. Markham said in a subdued voice and went on with her sorting.

She presently finished with the old-fashioned pictures and began to gather them together again. "Well," she said, straightening up, "there does not seem to be anything missing here. I suppose there might be some relative or distant connection that I'm forgetting but I really don't think so."

"Let's put all this stuff away then," Barbara said, beginning to gather up the scattered photographs.

When they had all been replaced Mrs. Markham announced that she was going straight to bed and advised us to do the same.

"What about Schmaltz?" Barbara asked, stretching and yawning.

Mrs. Markham said, "Oh dear! I had forgotten—and I'm so tired."

"We can talk to him," I suggested. "We'll tell him that as far as we can make out, nothing at all is missing. He'll love it."

Mrs. Markham smiled, "I'd appreciate it if you would. But don't stay up too late, girls. You're both worn out."

Barbara kissed her good night and went out. We found Schmaltz waiting downstairs and we gave our report with a certain amount of gusto.

He didn't say anything at all for a while. He merely put his mouth into a straight line and cracked every one of his knuckles while Barbara and I watched, fascinated.

Kate appeared when he got to the last knuckle, and she seemed to be pleased about something. She walked up to Barbara and announced with every sign of satisfaction, "The grocer didn't send no bacon, and we ain't got any for breakfast."

Barbara groaned, and the two of them went off to the kitchen while Schmaltz stared after them gloomily. "Everything's shaping up swell," he muttered. "Not one single person in this house has lost a book or a photograph, and there's no bacon for breakfast."

"What about Miss Giddens?" I asked.

"How the hell are you gonna find out if she's lost anything? Even she don't know."

"I could go up and have a try at her," I suggested.

"Go ahead," he said indifferently. "I guess you got plenty of time to waste."

I went up to Miss Giddens' room and found her standing before the mirror in her nightgown. She had a hat on her head and was thoughtfully regarding it from every angle.

I took a step forward and gasped. There was no mistaking the hat. It was Neville's.

CHAPTER TWENTY-SIX

MISS GIDDENS CAUGHT SIGHT of me through the mirror and turned around. "Good morning," she said politely.

"Where did you get that hat?" I asked.

She raised her hand uncertainly and touched it. "My hat?"

"Yes, your hat. That one you have on your head now. Where did you get it?"

"It's mine," said Miss Giddens. "He gave it to me, you know."

"Who?" I asked, hardly daring to breath.

She turned back to the mirror and nodded at her reflection. "He said I might have it, but he told me I must use it as a nightcap—wear it in bed, you see. He thinks it is not suitable for the street. Very rude to criticize a gift, I'm sure, but I wish I had a new hat for the street."

Uncle Alvin was back, then, if he had ever gone away. I felt pretty sure about it. I recognized his way of talking to Miss Giddens—the quiet, kindly manner he had with her. They had always got along very well, and he had been able to control her better than anyone else.

I shut my teeth firmly together to keep them from chattering and glanced around the large, untidy room. I felt that it was possible he was still hiding in there somewhere and I made a quick search. It did not take long: he was not crouching behind any of the furniture, and the only object under the bed, although not unlike Miss Giddens' street hat in general outline, was a strictly utilitarian piece of pottery.

The door connecting with Mary's room was still locked, and there was no sign of the missing key. The closet door was locked too. I pulled at it and rattled the knob, and wondered all the time whether Alvin were standing on the other side, holding his breath. I called his name softly, a couple of times, but there was no response. There was no key in the lock, and with a confused realization that Alvin must have locked the door from the inside if he were in there, I knelt down and put my eye to the keyhole. But it was too dark to see anything, and I had no matches with me. I knew, too, that Mrs. Markham never allowed Miss Giddens to have matches under any circumstances.

I sighed impatiently and stood up. "Is the gentleman in here?" I asked.

"I beg your pardon?" said Miss Giddens.

"Is the gentleman in this closet?"

She padded over and tried the closet door but when it would not open she lost interest and, without paying further attention to me or the closet, she got into bed and pulled the blankets up around her neck. Neville's hat fell off her head and rolled onto the floor. I left the room and went straight downstairs with the virtuous intention of laying the whole thing before Dodd or Schmaltz, only to find that apparently they had left, taking their chorus with them.

I peered cautiously into the drawing room and saw that Papa's bridge game was in full cry. He was partnering Neville and was telling Neville firmly but kindly that he had made a complete hash of playing the last hand. Neville had a "yes sir" sort of expression on his face, and Grace and Mary looked about as usual when playing bridge with Papa, like cats with saucers of cream in their tummies and more in sight. Grace was chewing gum.

Camille was sitting just behind Papa, humming a little song to herself, and Barbara was a short distance away, busily writing in a notebook.

I backed out quietly because I did not want to tell them about Alvin. After all, he might be hiding from one of them. I recognized the possibility that he was the murderer, but somehow my instinct was against that theory. In any case, I felt that I should tell the police before I told anyone else what I knew and suspected.

I wandered through the empty dining room and on to the kitchen, where I found Dennis pacing the floor and smoking a cigarette. Evie and Kate had gone.

"Still eating?" I asked, perching myself on one of the tables and idly swinging my legs.

"No," said Dennis, giving me scant attention. "I wanted to get away from it all."

"All what?"

"Your father, mostly," said Dennis. "He doesn't know how to conduct himself at a bridge table."

"No," I said, "but he knew how to conduct you out of his factory. Anyway, the drawing room is a public hall—he has a right to talk there if he wants to."

Dennis stopped pacing and leaned up against the sink. "Other people have a right to speak in the public halls, too," he said, regarding me through the smoke of his cigarette. "But your old man doesn't give anyone a chance."

"That's nonsense," I said carelessly. "You merely have to raise your voice and then jump in when he pauses for breath."

"Impossible," said Dennis coldly. "He never pauses for breath. And when I left he was talking the sheerest rubbish. Telling Neville how to play bridge, when he doesn't know himself."

I opened my eyes in astonishment. "Papa doesn't know how to play bridge?"

"No," said Dennis. "He's particularly and peculiarly foul."

"How would you know?"

Dennis disposed of his cigarette and immediately lighted another. "Because it so happens that I'm a very good player, myself."

"Oh," I said. "Do you keep your trophies under Miss Giddens' bed?"

He looked slightly mystified and explained with a touch of pride that his trophies were all at home.

"Why don't you go to bed and forget your troubles?" I asked.

"I'm waiting for a phone call—and the best place to wait for a phone call in a boardinghouse is right near the phone."

"Who's calling you?"

"Sometimes," said Dennis, "you're every bit as rude as your father."

"Oh no—Papa is in a class by himself," I explained simply. "But speaking of phone calls, how can I get in touch with Dodd or Schmaltz?"

"Go out and attack the cop on the beat," he suggested. "Why?"

"Oh well"—I slipped off the table—"I'm not so sure, just yet. Have you any matches?"

He handed me a book in silence, and I said, "Thank you," and left the kitchen.

I went straight up to Miss Giddens' room and was slipping through her door before I noticed that Dennis was right at my heels.

"What do you want?" I asked crossly.

"Just looking, thanks," he said, resting a shoulder against the jamb.

I hesitated and then decided to go on with what I wanted to do. Neville's hat was still lying on the floor beside the bed, and I kept my eyes away from it because I didn't want Dennis to notice it. I went straight over to the closet and tried to look into the keyhole with the aid of a lighted match. It was not very satisfactory, but as far as I could make out, there was no key on the other side. I stood up and looked at the blank surface of the door for a moment and then I stretched a tentative hand and turned the knob—and the door swung open! But the closet was empty, except for the collection of rubbish that Miss Giddens kept there.

I was sure, then, that Alvin had been hiding there. I remembered Miss Giddens saying, "Good afternoon," into the closet, and although there could not have been anyone there at that time, since Barbara and I had just looked, it seemed to indicate that Miss Giddens had expected someone to be there. And then she had said to Schmaltz, "He's in my bedroom," when Schmaltz supposed she was speaking of Neville.

And the muffled figure in the hall that had frightened me so. We had put the drape in the closet, and he must have wrapped himself in it in case he was seen. Probably he had been trying to get up to his room for something.

I walked over to the connecting door and found that it was still locked. I went around to Mary's side, but the key was not there, either, and I felt sure that Alvin had it.

Dennis was still with me. I looked at him and said impatiently, "What about your phone call? Hadn't you better go down and wait for it?"

"I really should," he admitted, "but you've no idea how intriguing it is to watch a young woman going slowly but surely batty. I think I'll stick around."

I made another effort to shake him. "Well, I suppose you know that Papa is always the first to reach the phone, and if someone asks for you he'll be only too happy to tell them that you're too drunk to talk."

"Oh well," said Dennis, "I suppose he's more to be pitied than blamed."

I left Mary's room and went all the way up to the fourth floor. I would not have had the courage if I'd been alone but since Dennis was still tailing me I was glad of the opportunity to try and find Alvin. I was uneasy about him and although I didn't exactly want Dennis to know that he was in the house I was anxious to find out if he were safe.

I searched the entire floor. None of the rooms was occupied except Evie's and Kate's. I got in there by asking them if I might have an aspirin. Evie was reading, and she looked up from her book and assured me that they had no aspirin. "I pinch the stuff from downstairs when I need one," she said.

Kate raised her head from her pillow and informed me that she had been asleep, that I had wakened her, and that it would be difficult, not to say impossible, for her to get off again.

I backed out and went downstairs.

"I've come to the conclusion," said Dennis, "that you're looking for something."

"Be that as it may," I replied airily, "we are now going to do your room."

Dennis' room was easy. There wasn't much in it, but I messed his things around as much as possible, in the hope that he would stay behind to tidy up again. But apparently he was not the tidy sort for he followed me out into the hall when I left.

I went straight to my own door. "I think I'll quit now," I said firmly. "Good-by." I went in, but he continued to tag at my heels and said, "Good-by," to the empty hall over his shoulder. He sat down on the painted chair and pulled out a cigarette.

I turned away from him with a sigh of exasperation, and my eye fell on the bureau.

A photograph was standing upright against the mirror—a photograph of a man. It was obviously an old one—postcard size and mounted on cardboard.

CHAPTER TWENTY-SIX

I STARED AT THE PHOTOGRAPH and felt goose pimples rise on my arms. Why should someone have burned several old pictures and yet saved one to put on my bureau where I would be bound to see it? It seemed completely senseless.

I picked the thing up and sat down on my bed and studied it. The man had darkish hair and mustache, light eyes, and a dimple in his chin, but although I looked at the face until my eyes ached I was forced to conclude that I had never seen him before and that the picture meant nothing to me.

Dennis shifted in his chair and asked, "What is it?"

"It's an old-fashioned photograph of a man," I explained absently. "But I don't know who it is or why it was left in my room."

Dennis got up and looked at it. "Are you sure you don't know who it is?" he asked after a moment.

"Quite sure. We have no dimpled chins in the family "

"When was it left here?"

"I don't know exactly," I said slowly. "Somewhere between the last time I was in here and now."

"I had more or less gathered that," said Dennis. "When were you last in here?"

"When I foolishly and hysterically imagined that I saw a ghost wrapped in the red drape."

"That wasn't very long ago," Dennis muttered, ignoring my bitterness.

I stood up. "I'm going to find out whether anyone in the house recognizes this."

We went out into the hall together and came face to face with Mrs. Markham, who narrowed her eyes and slightly compressed her mouth.

I realized that Dennis' presence in my room was an infringement on the rules of an orderly house and I made an effort to fix things. "Oh, Mrs. Markham, my window is sticking dreadfully. I had to ask Mr. Livingstone to close it for me."

Dennis gaped at me, completely mystified, but Mrs. Markham nodded, and her face relaxed into lines of weariness. "I'll have it seen to tomorrow, Diana." She pressed her fingers against her temples for a moment and sighed. "I simply cannot sleep. I've just had a hot bath and I'm hoping that will put me off. I'm desperately tired too."

"I'm sorry," I said. "Isn't there something you could take?"

She shook her head and murmured, "I don't know."

I showed her the photograph, then, and asked her if she knew who it was.

She took it from me and smiled almost immediately. "Where in the world did this turn up from? It belonged to Imogene Rostrum—he was a beau of hers. I believe she was quite sweet on him at one time and she kept the photograph. I remember she showed it to me once or twice, poor soul!"

"Then why was it in my room?" I asked helplessly.

"I'm sure I don't know." She gave it back to me and asked, "What are you going to do with it?"

"I suppose I'd better hand it over to the police."

"I think you should," Mrs. Markham agreed. "But I believe they've gone, haven't they?"

I nodded. "Perhaps I'd better get in touch with them."

"Oh, it'll keep," Dennis said. "Give it to them in the morning. They won't be able to make head or tail of it anyway."

"I think that's sensible, dear," said Mrs. Markham. "Keep it in your room. I shouldn't show it around too much because you don't know what it may mean to someone, and you can give it to the police in the morning."

She said good night to us, then, and went off to her room, and I went back and put the photograph in my bureau drawer. Dennis followed me and went straight over to my window. He opened and shut it a couple of times and then turned an accusing eye on me. "It works perfectly."

"I really don't know how you get along without your mother to guide you," I said impatiently. "Don't you know that you must be very careful with boardinghouse keepers, or they're apt to brand you with a scarlet *A* and throw you out into the snow?"

He laughed for quite a while after that and said at last, "So you pulled the wool over her eyes."

"Why are you following me all over the place, anyway?" I asked sharply. "I thought the situation summed up to the fact that I am snub-nosed and you have not the slightest interest in me."

"True," said Dennis. "You are snubnosed, and I have not the slightest interest in you."

I went to the mirror and stared critically at my reflection.

"I could have the snub removed," I said musingly, "but personally, I think it suits me."

"One woman's opinion," said Dennis. "Now I think—"

But I did not want to hear what he thought, so I left the room and started downstairs.

I gave up any further thought of looking for Alvin at that point. I admitted to myself that I was scared and I decided to tell the police all about it and let it go at that.

But I was interested in the photograph and I wondered whether Barbara could tell me anything more about Imogene's beau.

The bridge game was still in session in the drawing room, and Barbara was standing, with a piece of paper in her hand, watching the play. Papa was momentarily silenced because Camille was leaning on his shoulder, playing with his hair. As soon as he saw me he gave me such a look of anguished entreaty that I leaped straight to his rescue.

"Camille," I called, "will you come here for a moment? I have something private to ask you."

Camille came at once, and the rest of them looked up in surprise, with the exception of Papa, who breathed a gusty sigh of relief.

Camille's eyes were snapping with interest, and I felt a bit at a loss until I thought of the photograph and asked her if she had put it in my room.

She declared that she had not and although I tried to drop it there she kept on asking questions in a high, squeaky, excited voice until she knew all about it—and two minutes later the whole room was discussing it.

Dennis came in at the height of the jabbering and shook his head at me. "Couldn't wait, could you, to get down here and tell everyone?"

"I'm being frightfully misjudged," I murmured, "but I can't explain now."

"Or ever," said Dennis.

Barbara wanted me to go straight up and get the photograph, but I refused. "Your mother told me not to go showing it around, and anyway, none of you would know him. Unless you're old enough to have seen a beau of Miss Imogene's."

This shut Camille up, but Barbara continued to insist. "Can't I go up and get it now, so that we can all look at it?"

"No," I said firmly and began to feel stubborn about the thing. "I won't have it brought down."

Barbara flounced away, looking offended. She said something about going to bed after she had put a baconless menu on the kitchen table for Kate to follow in the morning.

I knew that she would go straight to my room to look for the photograph and I wished that I had locked the door, until I remembered that my key was missing. I had noticed that it was gone and supposed that Barbara had taken it for someone else since I was insisting on a bolt for my door. I felt a spasm of anger, and Papa, seeing me frown, ordered me to go to bed.

"What do you mean, go to bed?" I asked.

"What I say. You're tired and cross and you need some sleep."

"Do you realize how old I am?" I demanded.

"No, I don't," said Papa, "and I never have and I never will. Particularly when you act the way you do."

He must have thought that was funny because he loosed a great, booming laugh. Everyone else was silent, and Dennis, who had seated himself beside Grace, stuck his fingers into his ears.

I turned away and saw that Barbara was beckoning urgently to me from the hall. I went out, with a backward glance at the bridge table. The game had absorbed them again, and they paid me no attention. I noticed that Camille had deserted Papa and was hovering on Dennis' outskirts.

"What's the matter?" I said to Barbara.

"Did you get anything out of Miss Giddens about whether she has lost any photographs?"

"No," I said. "I—well, I didn't get around to it." I felt reluctant to tell her of my suspicions that Alvin was in the house.

"You should have then," Barbara said. "She just caught me in the hall and told me that the book the gentleman gave her has been stolen."

CHAPTER TWENTY-SEVEN

BARBARA AND I STARED at each other, and after a moment I said helplessly, "But who would go to the trouble of burning one of Miss Giddens' books?"

"No—wait a minute," Barbara said suddenly. "Miss Giddens said the gentleman had given her a book, remember? I'll bet that was the one that was burned."

I shook my head in an effort to clear it. "A gentleman gives Miss Giddens a book—and my guess is that she hasn't read one in twenty years—and another gentleman, lady, or perhaps just one of the masses takes it away and burns it in the furnace."

Barbara nodded. "Right. Now let's go up and see if the old Giddens has lost a photograph."

We started upstairs, and I asked conversationally, "Did you get as far as my room and see the picture of Miss Imogene's beau?"

"No," she replied absentmindedly. "I was on my way there when I ran into Miss Giddens in the hall."

"Does she ever read books or anything?"

Barbara shook her head. "She never reads anything—hasn't for years. I don't know whether it's her eyes or whether her mind can't take it in—both, I guess. Sometimes she picks up a book and sits there, turning the pages and looking around the room, and all the time the book's upside down and back to front."

We went into Miss Giddens' room and found her trying to throw her shawl out of the window. We rushed her, and Barbara grabbed the shawl while I closed the window.

"Near thing," Barbara commented.

Miss Giddens made a vexed sound with her tongue and attempted to raise the window, but we led her firmly away.

"Miss Giddens, won't you show us your photograph album?" Barbara asked formally.

Miss Giddens blinked several times and appeared to be mildly astonished. After apparently thinking it over for a while, she said, "Yes, my dear, certainly. Only too happy."

We waited for a bit, and then Miss Giddens said politely, "Is there anything I can do for you, my dear?"

"Your photograph album," Barbara said patiently. "May we see it?"

"Very glad you enjoyed it," said Miss Giddens. "Pray don't bother to put it away—we always leave it on the parlor table."

We started to look for the album ourselves, then, without bothering further with the formalities. Rather to my surprise, we found it almost at once. It was in one of the bureau drawers, along with a rabble of old ribbons and laces and artificial flowers. Miss Giddens, edging in between us, fingered one of the flowers and said, "Very pretty. I used to wear them, you know, and they looked very sweet."

Barbara carried the album to a table. "I knew she had one. When she first came here it was a hobby with her. She used to ask everyone for a picture to put in it—I know Mama gave her some. But I guess she had most of her faculties at that time."

The album was big and heavy, and there was a great variety of old pictures. Some were dated in the early nineteen hundreds, and there was a more modern collection of abominations. The book was completely filled, and we went through it very carefully, and toward the end we came upon a blank oblong where a post-card-size picture had been torn out.

We went through the remaining pages, and then Barbara closed the book and drew a long breath. "That's that then. But there's only the one missing and there were certainly more than one in the furnace."

I nodded. "But what about the one in my room? Maybe it came from here."

Barbara shook her head. "I don't think so. Miss Imogene wouldn't pass around pictures of her beaux—she'd keep them tucked away in lavender and old lace."

We heard the contingent from the drawing room coming up the stairs and making enough noise to lift the roof. I realized with shame that Papa was responsible for most of it and I said helplessly, "I'm glad he lives on the second floor, or he'd certainly wake your mother, and she needs her sleep."

"Well, yes," Barbara said, "but Mama is used to sleeping through all sorts of noise. Don't go out," she added quickly, as I started for the door. "Wait until they've gone to their rooms, and we'll go down and get something to eat."

"Thank you very much," Miss Giddens said unexpectedly. "Refreshment would be very welcome—I am a little hungry."

"Oh, you're just saying that to be polite," Barbara murmured.

It was some time before the din in the hall died down. They were telling each other what the government ought to do, with Papa well in the lead, Mary making a valiant second, Grace forcing in a word or two, and Neville's soprano invariably cut off at birth. Camille was talking steadily and continued to do so, no matter who had the floor.

Barbara had her ear against the door, impatiently waiting for them to disperse, and standing behind her, I noticed that Neville's hat was still lying on the floor where Miss Giddens had dropped it. I felt a sudden pang of conscience because I had not told the police about it. I should have got in touch with them—or told someone. I felt sure that Alvin was in the house—he must have been in the closet. But where was he now? Where could he be?

I felt undecided about whether to tell Barbara or not and, still thinking it over, I edged closer to the hat and kicked it under the bed. Miss Giddens immediately got down on her hands and knees and fished it out. I took it away from her and threw it under again and then I had to steer her away to the other side of the room. She went reluctantly and kept looking back over her shoulder at the bed.

Barbara turned away from the door, at that point, and said, "Okay. They have the government all cleaned and pressed and they've gone to bed. Let's eat."

We went out and found that Miss Giddens had donned her shawl and was sticking closer to us than the paper on the wall. Barbara groaned and led her back, and we put her to bed. We had to put her to bed three times in all, and the way we got her off at last was by pretending to sleep, ourselves, in a couple of chairs.

We crept out and started down the stairs and we had not gone half-way when I had an attack of jitters. "Let's not bother," I said, hanging onto the banisters and speaking through chattering teeth. "We shouldn't be hanging around down in those great, empty spaces at night. We ought to be in our beds. And you have to give me my key back."

"Don't be silly," said Barbara. "I have to go down anyway, because they've left all the lights on."

They had, and I mentally cursed them for a bunch of thoughtless incompetents as I followed Barbara down.

We went around the drawing room and turned all the lights off, and Barbara said abruptly, "Camille probably took your key. She wanted one and she knows that your key fits her door."

I said, "For God's sake, what kind of a hotel is this? Everybody snitching keys and all the keys opening anybody's door."

"This is not a hotel," said Barbara firmly. "It's a boardinghouse. And in a boardinghouse it is not considered cricket for the boarders to lock their doors against each other."

"I never heard of such foolishment," I said, turning off the last light.

When we reached the kitchen we found the light on and Dennis sitting there munching a sandwich. He glanced at us and said casually, "Hello, girls. Sit down—I'd like to have a word with you."

"Thank you, I'm sure," said Barbara.

Dennis raised one eyebrow. "Sarcasm? Well, I admit it's your kitchen and I suppose you think I'm eating extra food for nothing."

"Oh no," said Barbara. "No indeed. Not when I catch you, you're not eating extra food for nothing."

I laughed, and Dennis said, "All right, shove it on my bill, just as long as you don't add my room number into the total."

Barbara began to make coffee, and presently Dennis asked, "Have you heard anything of your uncle?"

Barbara's face clouded, and she replied with a faint sigh, "No, I wish we would."

I shifted uncomfortably and had almost made up my mind to tell them what I knew when Dennis said, "I understand the police are going over the city with a fine-tooth comb."

"I don't believe he's far away, if he's all right," Barbara said unhappily. "He always hated traveling around—he was happier at home."

I said, "Yes, that's right," without thinking, and although Barbara took no notice Dennis gave me an odd look.

"Did you find out anything about the book and photographs that were burned?" he asked presently.

Barbara nodded. "Miss Giddens."

"Don't be silly," said Dennis.

"We looked through her album," I explained, "and a photograph had been torn out. Only one though."

"Only one," Dennis repeated. "Must be the one that was propped on your bureau. But if so, why?" He turned to me. "Did it show any signs of having been torn out of something?"

I hadn't noticed and said so, and Dennis stood up abruptly. "Well, come on, girls, let's go up. I can't leave you down here."

We made our way quietly to the third floor and separated to our various rooms.

I was very tired and I got into bed, accompanied by a grim determination to go to sleep and forget everything.

The first thing I remembered was my missing key, and I lay there for a while, fighting an urge to run to Papa and tell him I was scared. I had begun to control myself and was growing calmer when I distinctly heard a faint noise in the hall. My eyes flew open, and my heart began to pound. I raised my head slightly from the pillow and in the heavy silence I heard a board creak.

Somebody was out there, then, and somebody who was trying to be quiet. I was in a panic by that time and I scrambled frantically out of bed because I was too terrified to lie there and die of fright. I stumbled to the door and pulled it open, and looked down an empty hall. The dim night light burned steadily; all the doors were closed, and the shadows were empty.

I mopped at my damp forehead with a shaking hand and glanced up at the light.

The gas jet had been turned on slightly.

CHAPTER TWENTY-EIGHT

I GASPED AND STOOD staring at the gas jet and did not even turn it off. And then a door opened down the hall, and I jerked my head away.

It was Dennis, and he was standing in his doorway looking at me. He made a hasty gesture for silence and came quickly down the hall and pushed me back into my room. He followed me in and closed the door silently. "What's going on out there?" he whispered. "We'd better try and find out—no sense in disturbing any of the others. What did you hear?"

I was still shaking and I said feebly, "Give me a cigarette and close the window."

He supplied the cigarette from my bureau, lowered the window softly, and seated himself on the painted chair.

"What did you hear?" I asked and wondered wildly whether it could have been Dennis who had turned on the gas.

He shifted impatiently, and the chair gave a despairing sort of creak. "I heard a board move in the hall and knew someone was walking across. I listened for a while, but there was nothing else until you opened your door, and then I wondered if something were wrong."

"How did you know it was my door that opened?" I asked, feeling clever.

Dennis grinned. "Sorry—no catch. Every door in the place squeaks, but yours has a little sigh all its own. I couldn't mistake it."

"But I opened it very quietly."

"Nevertheless," said Dennis, "it always sighs. Now tell me what you heard—beside that loose board."

"What makes you think I heard anything else?"

He said, "Oh, come down off your suspicious horse, can't you? I think that murdering maniac is on the prowl again, and we ought to do something about it."

I told him, then, about the gas jet and the slight noise I had heard at first but I added that in my opinion he should get in touch with the police, instead of wandering around the house by himself. He went straight out to the gas jet and examined it and then he shut it off and came back into my room. "Odd," he muttered, talking more to himself than to me. "No sense to it—it wasn't even turned full on."

"I found it that way once before," I told him.

He shook his head, and his forehead wrinkled into a frown. "Damned if I understand it—but there must be some reason for twice turning a gas jet half on."

"Maybe it's just Miss Giddens," I suggested.

"I don't think so. I doubt if she'd do the same thing twice, and she certainly wouldn't make any effort to be quiet about it."

I shivered, and he glanced at me. His eyes lost their speculative look and became intimate and warm. "Don't be frightened," he said, patting my shoulder. "I'll go down and get one of the cops from outside. Whatever is afoot for tonight had better be stopped, if possible. You stay here and don't go to sleep until I come back and tell you that the police are in the house."

"All right, but hurry. And get them in right away," I said, thinking of Alvin.

He departed quietly, and I stood at my door and heard him go down the stairs. After his footsteps had died away

I strained my ears to hear the opening of the front door, but the silence was heavy and blank.

I moved restlessly over to the bed and sat down and had another cigarette and after that I went back to the door and listened again, but there was no sound. I stood about twenty minutes of that, until I could stand it no longer, when I left my room and started quietly down the stairs.

I noticed a faint odor of gas and supposed that it had come from the half-opened jet.

The hall on the second floor was in darkness, but Miss Giddens' door was open and her room lighted. I looked in fearfully, half expecting to see Alvin, but instead, Miss Giddens sat in the rocking chair, looking at her album which Barbara and I had left on the table. She wore her long black winter coat over her nightgown and she looked up at me and said, "Good evening. Is dinner ready? They are always so late with dinner."

I gave a sympathetic murmur and glanced around the room. The closet door was ajar, and I went over and looked in, but it was empty except for the rubble of clothing. On my way out I looked under the bed, but of course Alvin was not there, and I felt a bit foolish.

I had reached the door when I remembered Neville's hat and I went back and looked under the bed again, but it had disappeared. I made a quick search through Miss Giddens' things and failed to find it. I even looked in the pottery under the bed while Miss Giddens observed, from behind me, "Very rude."

I went out, leaving Miss Giddens rocking herself with the album on her knees, although she was no longer looking at it and seemed to have forgotten me as well.

I went downstairs and found the lower hall dimly lighted and silent. I wondered where Dennis was and I began to get frightened again. He had come down to get a policeman, and yet there was no sign of him or anyone else. The front door was locked and bolted and the drawing room deserted. I moved on through the dark dining room on wobbly legs and gave a little gasp of relief when I saw that the kitchen was lighted. I plunged through the swing door and came to a wavering stop when I found that the place was deserted.

Where was Dennis, and what on earth had happened to him? I was on the point of running howling to Papa when I noticed that the cellar door was open.

I crept to the head of the stairs and peered down but I could see nothing and after a moment of wild indecision, I called, "Dennis!" in a high, shrill voice.

He said, "Hush!" immediately and added, "Come on down."

I stumbled down the stairs with relief pouring over me and made my way to where Dennis stood in front of the furnace.

"Something burning," he said briefly. "Looks like a hat."

I nodded and murmured, "Neville's hat, of course."

Dennis jerked around to look at me and asked sharply, "What do you mean?"

"Nothing," I said hastily, "nothing. Just nothing at all."

He put a firm hand on my arm and shook me.

"What do you mean, 'nothing'? Why the devil are you keeping things to yourself? Do you know that that was Neville's hat?"

"None of your damn business," I said and felt better than I had all the evening. "I'll tell the police what I know."

I pulled my arm away and went back up the stairs, but when I reached the kitchen Dennis was right behind me.

He took me by the shoulders and pushed me into a chair. "You should make an earnest effort to control that temper of yours. It gets you nowhere, really, and if you'll take a look at your father you'll see how an unchecked temper can blossom."

"I've taken a look at my father," I said, "and I've seen a man who does as he pleases when he pleases—and I can't see that that's such a bad end for anybody."

"You are a muddled thinker," said Dennis and gave me up. "About the police—I could not find one outside or in. But if that's Neville's hat in the furnace then either Alvin has been or still is in the house again, and in that case, it's imperative that he be found."

"Then we ought to whistle for Schmaltz or somebody," I said promptly. "If there's a search to be made they should make it."

Dennis looked at me and said after a moment, "I don't believe you trust me."

"Why should I?"

He laughed and raised himself from the edge of the table where he had been sitting. "You're quite right, of course, and I'll get in touch with them. Only I'd like to have something definite to tell them. You are sure it was Neville's hat in the furnace?"

"I think so," I said frankly. "I do know that Neville's hat was in Miss Giddens' room earlier this evening and that it has disappeared."

He nodded and said, "All right, that'll do."

I followed him to the telephone and moved around him uneasily while he made his call. When he had hung up at last he said, "All right, they're coming. Let's go back to the kitchen."

"Why?"

"More cheerful," he said and linked arms with me. When we reached the kitchen he dropped my arm and made straight for the ice chest.

I dropped into a chair and yawned. "Still trying to stuff your hollow leg?"

He turned around with a cold sausage in his hand and said, "Don't be rude."

"That's the second time I've been called rude tonight."

"Why?"

"I was looking for Neville's hat in a portable john."

He said, "I beg your pardon?" rather feebly, and I shook my head and yawned again.

There was a short silence, and then he said, "You're not a bit like your father, really."

"Why?"

"I don't know. One thing, I'd like to kiss you and I certainly wouldn't like to kiss your father."

"Very odd," I said coldly, "but then, of course, in a kissing position you would not be able to see my snub nose, would you?"

He said, "I don't know—let's see," and kissed me until I thought my front teeth would fall in.

I got away at last, because the doorbell rang. I flew to the front stairs and called over the banisters, "I don't want to see Schmaltz—you talk to them."

Dennis protested, but I went on up without looking back. Miss Giddens' light was still on, and she was still in the rocker. Ordinarily, I would not have given her a second glance, but something odd about the figure caused me to falter, and I looked again.

The eyes were protruding in a fixed stare, and they were not black, but blue.

CHAPTER TWENTY-NINE

I TOOK A STEP TOWARD the door and was conscious of a queer, dull wonder that I could ever have mistaken that ghastly figure for Miss Giddens. The face was darkly suffused, and the white hair was short. The long, dark overcoat was that of a man, and there were trousered legs at the bottom.

I turned and fled down the stairs, sobbing all the way. I could see Dennis and Schmaltz at the bottom, staring up at me, and I collapsed onto the lowest stair and pointed up because I could not get any coherent words out. Schmaltz went up the stairs like a buffalo, but Dennis bent over me and asked, "What is it? What has happened?"

I dropped my head onto my arms, still wailing, and after a moment Schmaltz appeared at the head of the stairs and called down to Dennis to summon a couple of men who were in a car at the curb. Dennis straightened up and went off, and presently the men brushed past me and went upstairs. Dennis pulled me up from the step, then, and took me into the drawing room. He established me in a chair, turned on a few lights, and left me, and I heard him hurrying up the stairs.

It was quiet enough in the drawing room, but I could hear plenty of activity from the second floor. I tried to ignore it, but my mind was overexcited and overactive. I kept thinking of things: the photograph in my room, the gas turned slightly on, Barbara's pin and Miss Giddens' book burning in the furnace, Neville's hat. The hat struck me as being funny, and I laughed until the tears came. Someone was phoning in the hall, and when he had finished he came in and looked at me.

"Hold it, lady," he said uneasily.

I thought that was funnier than the hat and I laughed even harder until Dennis came into the room. He walked straight up to me, slapped my face, and said loudly, "Shut up!"

I stopped laughing, flew out of my chair, and hit out wildly. Dennis ducked, but Schmaltz's henchman got it.

He said with a touch of bitterness, "Good shot, lady," and went gloomily from the room.

"Sit down," said Dennis, "I'm going to make you some coffee." He pushed me back into my chair and went off.

"How do you know I want coffee?" I called after him, but he took no notice, and I figured that he probably wanted the coffee himself.

He returned almost immediately and announced, "It's on."

"Is it—Uncle Alvin—up there?" I asked miserably.

"Yes. Same condition," he said briefly. "Gas and a bump on the head."

"Why the—why were they all hit on the head?" I whispered.

"Very obvious," said Dennis, hunching his shoulders. "They were put out first, so that they would lie quietly while being gassed."

Quite a crowd of men came in at the front door just then and went upstairs, and at the same time Mary came down, draped in her fancy negligee.

"Has anyone a cigarette?" she asked grimly.

Dennis produced one, and Mary observed, "We are being picked on one by one. Interesting to know who's next."

"Poor Mrs. Markham," I sighed. "This will ruin her."

Mary said, "I'm afraid so. It seems to me the best thing she can do is break the place up into apartments and redecorate."

"Still the same rooms though," I said gloomily. "Is she up there now?"

Mary nodded. "She and Barbara are in Grace's room. Grace is doing the comforting job—she's good at that."

There was a short silence, and then I said, "I wonder how he got back into the house."

Dennis shook his head. "It's queer, that; Miss Giddens insists that he came in with her."

"Came in with Miss Giddens?" I said, puzzled. "When?"

"Nobody knows," Dennis explained. "But she keeps repeating 'he came in with me and stayed. We had a nice walk.' "

"Why, yes," I said slowly, "as a matter of fact, she told me she had been for a walk that night. She said she had not slept and so had gone out for a walk. Perhaps she really did, after all."

"But there were police all over the place," Mary protested. "Surely one of them must have seen her if she did go."

"Why don't you go up and ask them?" I suggested.

"Don't be silly."

"Go on up and try," Dennis urged her. "Put a lot of schoolteacher into it, and they'll answer you before they have time to think."

Mary stood up. "Oh well—I suppose they can only throw me down-stairs."

She went off, and a moment later Papa appeared, fully dressed.

"Is it absolutely goddam necessary for you two to stick together every minute of the day and night?" he shouted. "Is there no one else in this ruddy house that you could pair off with?"

"Must you think of your own affairs, even at a time like this?" I asked.

He threw himself into a chair and nearly broke it. "Why the hell can't you stay at home and sew or something."

"And you'd be the first one to bawl me out for spoiling my eyes," I snapped.

Dennis said, "Why can't you stop worrying about yourselves and think of the spot Mrs. Markham is in? She'll never be able to carry on here. You ought to buy the house from her, Prescott, so that she can make a fresh start somewhere else."

"I'd sooner buy Pikes Peak," Papa said savagely.

Mary came back and sat down with us.

"Miss Giddens did go out for a walk," she said, "early in the morning after Alvin had disappeared, at about five o'clock. One of the policemen saw her and figured that she was harmless. But no one saw her come back, and they think that Alvin simply walked in with her and somehow missed being seen. Though why he should come right back after leaving, I don't know, and Schmaltz doesn't know either."

"I think he was afraid to check in at a hotel," I said slowly. "Mrs. Markham said something of the sort, and I believe she was right. He was a self-conscious, retiring sort of man, so he just crept home and hid himself."

Schmaltz appeared just then and put us through a round of questioning. Halfway through it, there was a strong smell of burning from the kitchen, and we all went out to find Dennis' coffee had burned away.

It was beginning to grow light by the time Schmaltz had finished with us, and since Papa had long since gone to sleep in his chair we left him there and went upstairs.

I did not expect to sleep but I went to bed and decided to rest, at least. But an idea about Miss Imogene's beau popped into my too restless mind, and I got up again to have another look at him.

Only he was not there. Someone had removed the photograph from my drawer.

CHAPTER THIRTY

I WENT BACK TO BED and gave up any thought of trying to sleep. I lit a cigarette and deliberately concentrated on the missing photograph. I felt pretty sure that it had come from Miss Giddens' album: it was the same size and it seemed highly probable. But why would anyone bother to steal it from me? And the photographs that were burning in the furnace had apparently come from nowhere. I wondered afresh why Imogene's beau had been placed in a conspicuous spot in my room, and quite suddenly I saw it. Uncle Alvin had done it. He was trying to get a message through to me, an important message. Something so important, in fact, that the photograph had promptly been stolen. And I had not caught on in time.

I put out my cigarette and made a determined effort to concentrate on the problem, and my next conscious moment was when I woke up at ten o'clock to find Evie in my room with a breakfast tray. She put it on my knees and said chattily, "This costs extra, you know, but I guess your old man don't worry about things like that. He said bring it up at eleven, but that would've thrown Kate and me out something terrible, so I didn't argue with him—you know how he is—I just waited as late as I could."

"All right," I said, "don't apologize."

"Who's apologizing?" she yapped shrilly. "I'm just tellin' you."

"What's going on downstairs?" I asked, pouring coffee.

"Things ain't so good," Evie said with mournful enjoyment. "Mrs. Markham, now, she's just given up. She's lyin' in bed, staring at the ceiling."

"It must be terrible for her," I said soberly. "I'm sorry. And yet, I'd have thought she'd be the last to collapse—she's so efficient."

"Yeah," Evie said, chewing vigorously. "Miss Barbara was down tryin' to see to things, but she kept busting out crying, and Kate made her go back to her room. I guess she's in there now."

I nodded. "I'll go in and see her as soon as I finish."

"Sure—only you're wanted by that Dodd, too. See? But your old man said you was to be let sleep, and Dodd had to give over. No one," said Evie, looking aggrieved, "ever said I was to be let sleep."

She went off reluctantly after a while, and I finished my breakfast and then went in to Barbara.

She was not crying, but her eyes were red and swollen, and her face looked a mess. I gave her a cigarette. "Here—you might as well do something besides lie on the bed and look at the floor."

She took the cigarette and said thickly, "We knew he was in danger, and we didn't help him."

I said, "Listen, Barbara, there's simply no sense in talking like that. We did our best, and that's all we could do."

She turned her head away without replying and looked at the wall.

"Did you take that photograph out of my room?" I asked.

"What photograph?"

"The one that somebody planted on my bureau. Miss Imogene's boy-friend."

"Oh, that," said Barbara. "No, I didn't take it. I never even got to look at it—and I meant to."

"Well, it's gone."

She turned her head back and looked at me. "Gone? Why? Who'd want to take it?"

"Who'd want to do any of all this?" I said bitterly. "The whole thing is crazy."

Barbara looked at the wall again, and I thought she was going to cry. I said hastily, "Don't just lie there and think of all those ghastly things. Get up and come downstairs and do things. Play bridge with Papa, even, but don't lie there."

She swallowed a couple of times and then pulled herself off the bed. "I guess you're right," she said slowly. "I ought to see to things anyway. Mama's out cold. I wanted to get the doctor for her, but she won't let me." She moved over to the mirror and began to touch up her face.

I stood behind her and nodded approval. "Get yourself spruced up—you'll feel a lot better."

But she broke down again almost immediately and cried on my shoulder. "Poor Uncle Alvin—he was such a dear—I can't stand it. And I'm frightened—there's something horrible in this house."

I managed to get her straightened out in about fifteen minutes and sent her downstairs with instructions to keep her hands busy and her mind a blank.

When she had gone I returned to my room and dressed slowly. I could not see any need for hurry since there would be nothing to do when I got down but answer questions put to me by Dodd and Schmaltz and try to look innocent under their suspicious eyes.

I was nearly dressed when Mrs. Markham came in. She looked dread-fully ill—her face white and drawn, with deep lines in her forehead and around her mouth. I helped her to my chair, and she leaned back and pulled her dressing robe around her.

"I don't know why I should have gone to pieces this way," she said tiredly. "I don't usually, you know."

"No, of course not," I said soothingly. "But this has been too much."

"I just wanted to ask you to give Barbara some help," she said, kneading her hands. "I don't mean physical help, naturally. But if you could talk to her—keep her cheerful. I'm afraid she'll have to carry on for a few days—I'm done."

"I'll see to her," I promised. "She'll be all right. But you must go back to bed."

I went with her to her room and helped her into bed. "You must try to relax," I said. "Don't worry about anything."

She turned her head restlessly on the pillow and muttered, "But I must worry—the funerals. Somebody must see to them."

"Kate will see to the funerals," I said firmly. "She'll do it the right way too, better than you or I could. There'll be no need for you to appear—you stay here and get your strength back. I'll see that everything goes all right."

She murmured, "You are very kind," and closed her eyes, and I went quietly out and left her. It seemed odd to see her stretched on her back and useless. She had always been so calm and efficient.

I went down to the drawing room where I found Papa sitting in a chair and drumming his fingers restlessly on the arm. Camille was telling him all about Uncle Alvin with mournful gusto, while Mary stared out of a window and said nothing. Grace was knitting.

I backed out and went on to the dining room. Dodd and Schmaltz were there and had Dennis up before them. I tried to creep through to the kitchen without being seen and had almost made it when Dodd spoke up crisply. "I should like to question you, Miss Prescott."

"All right," I said, edging on. "I'll be in the kitchen when you want me." I slipped into the kitchen, half expecting them to call me back, but they didn't.

I found Barbara wearing her coat and hat and conferring with Kate over a list. She glanced at me and said, "Everything has been so upset for the last few days that we haven't done the proper ordering. I'm going out to get a few essentials at the delicatessen. Want to come along?"

"I can't. Dodd wants to question me."

"Dodd's a pest," she said and started for the door. I was reminded of how she frequently had to change books for the Rostrums and I said suddenly, "Hey! Did you ever take the Rostrums' last book back to the library?"

She paused, with her hand on the door knob, and said, "No—no, I didn't. I wonder if anyone else did?"

"Is the place open on Sunday?"

She nodded. "I think so—it's a paper-and-tobacco shop."

"Then find out if anyone had returned it and if not get a copy of the same book if they have it. If it hasn't been returned I'll bet anything it was the one that was burned in the furnace."

Barbara opened her eyes very wide. "Why, I believe you're right. With all our searching we never came across it."

"Maybe the police have it," I said doubtfully.

"I don't think so. Anyway I'll stop in at the library."

She went off, and I went down to the cellar. I had made up my mind to get a key for my door and I remembered that Barbara had once taken some keys from a dusty old bureau down there. I found the thing and jerked open a drawer. There were no keys in it, but a couple of old, framed photographs lay under a film of undisturbed dust. I picked them up and saw that one was a class picture, with the kids staring like a bunch of dead fish in the usual manner.

The other was the same print of Miss Imogene's beau that had been left in my room.

CHAPTER THIRTY-ONE

THE FRAME WAS BADLY TARNISHED and the glass cracked and dusty. I stared at it for a long time and as I stood there I began to get the first glimmerings of the truth.

I shivered and dropped the photographs back into the drawer with a clatter. I was up in the kitchen before I remembered that I had not looked for a key, but I would not go down again.

Kate was fizzing like soda water because she said the lunch was all ready, but they could not even get the tables set since the police were still holding out in the dining room.

"Leave it to me," I said airily. "I'll take charge."

I went into the dining room and found that Grace was being put through it. She was saying, "I really don't know," with one of her stubborn looks.

"You gentlemen staying for lunch?" I asked loudly.

They produced a pair of formidable frowns, and I frowned back. "We're having a few tasty extras from the delicatessen, and it won't cost you much. Only you'll have to move into the drawing room and give us a free hand."

"What's she talking about?" Dodd said irritably. "Now I'm all mixed up here."

"I want you to move into the drawing room," I explained, beginning to be irritable, myself, "or allow the waitress to set the tables. We have to eat."

"Well, who's stoppin' her?" Schmaltz asked, aggrieved.

Dodd said, "Certainly. Tell her to come in and get started. And will you come here, please, Miss Prescott? I wish to ask you some questions." I nodded and after telling Evie to go ahead, I seated myself in front of them and opened the proceedings by telling them about the picture in the cellar. Schmaltz was sent off to get it, and Dodd fired questions at me, which were mostly the same things over and over again. Schmaltz presently puffed up from the cellar with the picture, and Dodd, after a brief glance at it, tucked it away into his leather case.

By the time they had finished with me and had reluctantly handed me over to Papa, the boarders were eating all around us. Mrs. Markham and Barbara did not appear, and Evie, enjoying her gum to the full since the eye of authority was absent, explained that she had taken up a tray for them. Miss Giddens finished her meal at about the time I started mine, and she pulled a chair up to our table and sat quietly watching Papa eat.

Papa squirmed and muttered, "Damn it, why can't she pick on someone else?"

I said, "Let her enjoy herself. I think it reminds her of when she was a little girl and went to the zoo."

There was a loud guffaw from behind us, where Schmaltz was eating his lunch, but when we turned around he was studying a spot of gravy on the tablecloth with deep attention.

"Someday I'm going to slap you down," Papa said to me in a fierce undertone.

Miss Giddens said, "Good afternoon."

"Good afternoon," I replied, and Papa asked peevishly, "Why do you bother to answer her? It only encourages her."

"How would you like to be a friendless old woman?"

Evie approached and asked, "Would you like a third helping, Mr. Prescott?"

I said, "No," and Papa and Miss Giddens said, "Yes," together, so Evie hurried off to get it.

Papa swept his napkin across his mouth and leaned over to me, creaking slightly. "You needn't let it get about, but I've pulled a few strings, and you and I are definitely going home tomorrow."

"Good."

"And I hope to God you've learned your lesson. If you'll stay there quietly for a while and behave yourself we might get down to Florida in January."

"I won't stay quiet and behave unless you bring Dennis home too."

He flung himself back in a fury and knocked over a glass of water, and it streamed across the table and poured down onto Miss Giddens' skirt. She looked at it, brushed it off a bit with a grubby handkerchief, and said, "Tch, tch."

Papa made an effort to lower his voice, and his face glowed with an angry red.

"Don't sit there and tell me you've fallen for that dumb jerk," he hissed savagely.

"I want him around," I said, "and that's all you need to know."

"Well, you can't have him, and that's flat."

"We'll see," I said pleasantly.

Papa leaned across the table again and creaked afresh. "Now listen, honey. I'll dig you up some good-looking men—I'll get you ten or a dozen. Just give me a couple of weeks."

"All right," I said, "but don't make it too obvious."

He heaved a vast sigh and relaxed. "That's fine, baby. Now let's go and play some bridge."

"Delightful," said Miss Giddens. "Very glad to."

We shifted to the drawing room, and I was relieved to see that they were all there—Mary, Grace, Camille, Neville, and Dennis. I felt sure that Papa could get a game out of that material without dragging me into it.

Barbara appeared from the hall and held up a book. "I was able to get it," she called. "The first one has not been returned, but they had another copy."

I went over and grabbed the book and said, "Hush! You don't have to tell everybody."

"Why?"

"Don't be foolish. If that was the book that was burned—and it seems almost certain that it was—" I paused, suddenly conscious that the room was very quiet, and turned around. They were all staring at us, and some of them had their mouths open. I had been speaking in a low voice but I knew they must have heard. I pressed the book against my side and left the room in a hurry. I went all the way up to my bedroom, and Barbara followed me.

"I'm sorry I didn't keep it quiet," she said in a subdued voice. "I didn't realize that it meant anything."

"It doesn't matter. You run along and leave me to it, Barbara. I want to read it."

"You going to read that great tome all the way through?"

"I read a big book before," I said, "and I got through it then."

"How long did it take you?"

"About fifteen years," I said, "but I'm going to try and cut this to ten if you'll go away and stop pestering me."

She said, "All right, I'm going, but I think you're biting off more than you can chew. I'll drop in from time to time and see if you've found anything."

She went off, and I made myself comfortable and dug in. The book was quite interesting, as a matter of fact—all about the workings of the human body and heredity and things like that.

I read it through from cover to cover without a single interruption, starting at about two-thirty and finishing shortly after six. I put it down then, closed my eyes to rest them, and thought about it over a quiet cigarette. I had to admit that I was puzzled. The Rostrums had read it, and Uncle Alvin had read it, and then someone had burned it—and yet I could not quite put my finger on anything.

I was convinced that Uncle Alvin had put the photograph on my bureau, after having torn it out of Miss Giddens' album, and he had been trying to tell me something. I moved my head restlessly, still baffled by any connection between the murders and Miss Imogene's beau.

I thought of the scare I had had when I had seen Alvin in the hall, wrapped in the drape. Thinking about it, I remembered that after I had flung back into my room, screaming, I had heard the door open, and that was some moments before the rest of them had appeared. He must have thrown the drape onto the newel post, then, and come after me to try and shut me up. But the others were close behind him, and he would have had to hide....

I sat up. He must have hidden right in my room—there would be no time to go out again. He had wanted desperately to tell me something, and I had gone on screaming like a silly parrot. I got off my bed and looked around the room. There was only one hiding place. The closet was far too small, and poor Alvin must have gone under the bed.

I knew that Evie's method was to clean only those parts of the floor that showed, and if my reasoning was correct there should be some marks of Alvin having been under my bed. I pulled it feverishly away from the wall and looked eagerly at the dust and fluff that had collected there.

I was right. The dust had been scuffed around, and a small piece of paper lay against the baseboard.

It was a snapshot of Miss Imogene's beau and Barbara, as a little girl.

CHAPTER THIRTY-TWO

IT WAS A CLEAR PICTURE, and there was no mistaking either of them. Barbara must have been about eight years old, and she wore the same little neat, starched gingham dress that I had seen in other pictures of her as a child.

I supposed the snapshot must have dropped out of Alvin's pocket when he hid under my bed—and later, when he discovered that it had gone, he had ripped the portrait out of Miss Giddens' album. But what message was I supposed to read into a picture of Miss Imogene's beau? I decided that she must have known him for some years, since he looked definitely older in the snap with Barbara than he did in the portrait.

Someone knocked on the door, and I hastily slid the snapshot under the pillow and called, "Come in."

Dennis walked in, nodded, and, looking past me, observed, "You've been reading."

I glanced at the untidy bed, with the book lying in the middle, and said admiringly, "How in the world did you guess?"

He walked over and picked the book up. "The Rostrums were reading it just before they died," he said in an absorbed voice and added sharply, "Where did you get it?"

"How do you know they were reading it?"

"I saw them with it," he explained impatiently. "Where did Barbara find this? It's the book she brought into the drawing room after lunch, isn't it?"

"I have to answer all the silly questions that Dodd and Schmaltz can think up," I said defiantly. "But I have both a thumb and a nose for yours."

He said, "Don't be vulgar. How about a sherry before dinner?"

"I'd be only too happy to offer you one, except that I have one glass which I use for my toothbrushes—and no sherry at all."

"Comb your hair," said Dennis, "and accompany me to my room. I was offering an invitation, not a hint."

"Well"—I glanced at my hair in the mirror and picked up my comb—"I could do with a sherry, at that. You run along and dig up a chaperon, and I'll be right there."

He said, "Right," and withdrew, and I cleaned myself up and then went along to his room.

I found Miss Giddens perched on the straight chair, eating candy, while Dennis stood at the bureau, pouring sherry. He put down the bottle when I came in and, closing the door behind me, enfolded me in a mighty embrace and kissed me several times.

"For God's sake," I said when I had got myself free. "What do you think you're doing?"

"It's quite all right. I thought that was why you wanted me to get a chaperon—so that we could do a little legal petting."

"Very funny," I said coldly. "I'd laugh, only I'm afraid I might split my side."

I picked up one of the glasses and sipped at the sherry. Miss Giddens, watching me with a candy poised in midair, said, "Thank you, my dear. I think it might keep out the cold, you know."

"She wants some sherry," I said to Dennis.

He shook his head. "This is a special import which I keep for heiresses and people of that sort."

"You know something?"

"Shoot," said Dennis.

"I think you've decided to marry me for what you can get out of it."

He nodded. "You're quite right—I have. And if you come right down to fundamentals that's what anybody marries for—what they can get out of it. In your case, you are getting a class-A exhibit and an upright and honorable character to boot."

"You are purposely confusing the issue," I said with dignity. "I mean what you can get out of it in cold cash."

"Yes—well, of course, there will be quite a lot, won't there? And when I get your nose fixed up and see to your clothes a little you won't be bad at all."

"If you think you can improve on the way I dress," I said furiously, "you're a conceited fool. In fact, you are anyway."

"Don't lose your temper over trifles," Dennis said amiably. "I'll have to break you of that."

I swallowed the rest of my sherry and simmered down. "Listen," I said after a moment, "the day you can get Papa's consent to our marriage I'll announce the engagement. But not before."

He set his glass down on the bureau, dropped a kiss onto the top of my head, and said, "Darling, it's as good as done. Let's go."

I extended my glass. "We'd better have another one before we approach Papa."

He picked up the bottle and said, "All right, but hurry. It's almost dinner time."

"Supper, on Sundays."

"Supper?" said Miss Giddens. "Thank you very much—enjoyable visit. Good afternoon." And she padded briskly out of the room.

"Now we've lost our chaperon," Dennis said. "You ought to be more careful. If anyone comes in you'll have to hide in the closet."

"No, I won't," I said, sitting down on the straight chair. "I'll face the music like a gentleman."

Dennis took my glass away, pulled me up from the chair, and said, "Come on, I can't wait any longer. I want to ask your father for your hand before supper."

He urged me out of the room, and I said resignedly, "All right, anything for a laugh. But you'll ruin his appetite."

He took my arm as we descended the stairs. "If there is anything in this wide world that can ruin that hog's appetite I haven't heard of it, and neither has he."

We found Papa in his room, sitting in one of the Victorian chairs that dotted it and looking depressed. He gave us an evil look and said to me, "Where have you been all day? Playing tag with that damn coat-and-suit ad? Take him out of my room!"

"I can't help it, Papa," I said meekly. "He's hunting a fortune, and I can't get rid of him."

Dennis wandered over to the bureau and smoothed his hair back with one of Papa's brushes.

"I hate to break this to you," I went on, "but I believe he's going to have the gall to ask you for my hand."

"I'll smack him all the way down the stairs if he does," Papa snarled.

Dennis straightened his tie, left the bureau, and seated himself on the edge of the bed. "Mr. Prescott, that was a very fine grand coup you pulled on Grace this afternoon."

Papa struggled with his face, but it looked blank in spite of himself.

"But perhaps," Dennis went on easily, "it was only a fluke. It may be that you did not know what you were doing."

"What the devil do you mean?" Papa bellowed. "I always know what I'm doing."

Dennis shook his head. "A very obvious Vienna coup turned up later, which you did not execute, so I suppose you really don't understand these plays."

"Do you?" asked Papa in a strangled voice, quivering from head to foot.

"Most certainly. Furthermore, I could teach them to you if you'll give your consent to the marriage of daughter and self."

Papa said, "I'll see you in hell first," but his voice was as mild as an April shower.

"All I want is your consent," Dennis said reasonably. "I'll attend to the rest, myself. And I'll teach you all those plays. You'll have the boys at the Elk's Club utterly confounded."

Papa actually seemed to be thinking it over, and I said in a small voice, "I thought you were going to smack him downstairs—I didn't dream you'd be so weak. I told him we'd be engaged if you gave your consent."

Papa glanced at me and said defensively, "You can always break your word. Like the time I gave you the red roadster if you'd give up smoking."

I turned around and made for the door in a temper. "All right, you rat. Sell me down the river, so you can catch a little prestige."

"Nobody can sell you down any river you don't want to go," Papa yelled after me.

I ran into Mrs. Markham in the front hall. She looked worried and anxious and still very ill, I thought. I asked her how she felt, and she said, "I think a little better. I felt I should come down tonight. It's Kate's evening off, and Evie cannot be trusted."

"Where's Barbara?"

"She's giving Evie a hand. Are the others coming down? The gong went some time ago."

"They're talking business," I said bitterly, "but I guess they'll be along."

I went on to the dining room and met Miss Giddens on her way out.

She turned around when she saw me and followed me in again.

Mary and Grace were talking in low tones, but the others were eating in silence. Papa and Dennis appeared after a while, but I could not tell from their expression whether I had been sold or not, and I was too proud to ask.

They all went into the drawing room after supper, but the atmosphere was pretty gloomy, and when Dennis brought out a pack of cards, laid them out in front of Papa, and winked at me I gave up and went to my room.

I found, to my surprise, that the bed had been neatly laid down. I remembered that it had been done the first few nights after my arrival there, but no one had bothered since.

"Funny," I thought uneasily, "that they should suddenly get fancy again, and on Kate's night off too."

I thought of the snapshot and jerked the pillow away but I was hardly surprised when I found that it had disappeared.

No one knew about my having found that snapshot though, so who-ever had come in must have come for another reason.

I lay down on the bed to think about it and I must have dozed, for I was brought suddenly to alert attention by the sound of the glass shade tinkling against the bulb out in the hall, and that meant that someone was turning the gas half on again.

CHAPTER THIRTY-THREE

I SCRAMBLED OFF THE BED and stood in the middle of the room for a mo-ment, breathing quickly, and then I crept over to the door and looked out into the hall. It appeared to be deserted, but someone could have been hiding in the shadows, and I backed into my room again and stood lean-ing against the closed door, trying to fight down a rising sense of panic.

Why should that gas be turned on again? Who were they after now? And suddenly it came to me with a fearful thud. It was I, of course. I had just finished the book, hadn't I?

I looked wildly around the room, but the book was gone. It was dan-gerous and so it would have to be burned, and I had read it and so I was dangerous too.

But why? What was it all about? The book had dealt with the human body and its workings and peculiarities, nothing that I had not known or read about before.

I began to feel a little less frightened. I didn't really know anything and so how could I be a menace to anybody?

I moved away from the door and stood hesitating, thinking of nothing, and quite quietly, like a curtain going up on a lighted stage, the whole dreadful explanation dropped into my mind.

I fell back against the door and stood shivering and drenched with fear. If I could get downstairs—but it was out there in the hall, waiting for me. And I could not even lock my door! But I'd have to lock it, somehow. I couldn't just wait there, with the door open, like an animal in a trap.

My eye fell on the bureau, and I drew a quick breath. I could push it in front of the door and wait until someone came up and then I could call out.

I straightened up, and at the same moment the knob turned, and there was a tentative push from the outside. I flung my weight against the door, and the pressure was released at once, and after a moment I heard quiet, receding footsteps.

I rested my wet forehead against the wooden panel and tried to think quietly. I might make a dash for the stairs, but I felt absolutely certain that I would be struck down on the way. And if I screamed my door would be brutally forced at once, and it would be the same thing. There would be just time enough before the others could get up from the drawing room.

I heard someone come up the stairs just then and on to the landing and I flung my door open with a gasp of relief, but it was only Miss Giddens. She blinked at me and walked into my room, and I closed the door quickly and leaned on it again.

I decided at last to make a supreme effort to get the bureau over in front of the door and then I could scream until my voice gave out. But at the same time Miss Giddens stood up and indicated that she wanted to leave.

I thought of something else and I whispered to her to bring me my purse. She brought it from the bureau, and I fished out an address book and pencil and wrote a frantic note to Dennis. I tucked it into Miss Giddens' bosom, told her to deliver it to Dennis, and promised that he'd give her some candy if she did. I opened the door a little, braced my foot against it, and let her slip out and then I shut it tightly again.

Miss Giddens was intercepted almost at once. I listened with my heart thudding, and it was only when the old lady padded off again that I realized that I could have used the time to move the bureau.

I left the door and flung myself at the awkward piece of furniture in the hope that there was still time, but I was just too late. The bureau was almost against the door when she slipped in.

I don't believe I felt very much of anything as we looked at each other.

"Can I help you?" she asked, edging toward me but keeping the door blocked.

I stared at her without answering and I seem to remember wondering, in a misty sort of way, how she intended to do it. She'd waste no time if I screamed, of course.

I saw then that she held an Indian club half behind her. So that was how she did it. She'd hit me on the head first and then leave me to die of the gas.

I moved back a step, and she said softly, "Don't be afraid—I'm through. I can't do it this time. Sit down and relax."

She backed toward the door, and I started to breathe again. She still had the door blocked, but I was well out of her reach.

"I just wanted to explain a little," she said quietly, "so that you will not judge me too harshly."

I eased myself onto the edge of the bed, still staring at her.

"It was unfortunate," she said haltingly and paused. She was looking at me intently, and the arm that held the club began to move up and out.

I realized it too late. I saw that she was going to throw the club, even as the thing came crashing against my forehead.

CHAPTER THIRTY-FOUR

WHEN I WOKE UP I was surprised, in a vague sort of way, to find myself surrounded by Papa, Dennis, and a trained nurse, instead of white satin and black wood. I was conscious of a bandage of some sort on my head.

Papa was seated on the painted chair, looking grim, and Dennis was sitting on the end of the bed. The nurse was trying to sit on the window sill, which was not wide enough, and she looked annoyed.

As soon as Papa saw that my eyes were open he shouted to the nurse. She drifted to my bedside and said, "All right. So what do you want me to do now?"

"Take her temperature," Papa yelled. "What about her pulse? Is she all right?"

The nurse said acidly, "She is in excellent condition."

I hushed Papa and said, "Listen, Nurse, go on out and find a comfortable chair and go to sleep. We'll call you if I start to die."

"Good idea," said Dennis and escorted her out of the room. He came back and sat on the side of my bed, although Papa tried to bar his way by sticking out his foot, but Dennis walked right over it.

"How do you come to be allowed into the sickroom?" I asked.

"Opportunity knocked," Papa said sourly, "and trust him to take advantage of it. He saved your life, and now we're obligated for the rest of our ruddy lives."

Dennis grinned from ear to ear, and I said impatiently, "Please tell me what happened. My head aches all the way down to my neck, and somebody is sure to give me a pill and put me to sleep pretty soon, but I must know what happened first. How did you catch her—where is she?"

"Mrs. Markham," said Dennis. "She's in custody. Barbara's going to some cousins out West."

I felt the tears come into my eyes and whispered, "Does Barbara know?"

Dennis nodded soberly. "She had to know. You see—"

"Why don't you start where opportunity knocked?" Papa asked jealously.

Dennis said, "Well, I began to get uneasy because you had been upstairs for so long and I decided to go up and see what you were doing. I thought I heard a noise on the landing as I was coming up to the third floor, but when I reached your room you were not there. I went informal, then, and simply walked into every room on the floor. When I reached Mrs. Markham's room I found that it was locked. She answered when I tried the door and even opened it a crack and told me in a tired voice that she thought she'd go to bed and try to sleep, and did I want anything. I said I wanted to talk to her and simply pushed past her into the room, although she put up a fight and hauled in outraged modesty in a last, desperate effort to keep me out.

"I found you on the floor in front of the gas log she has in the fireplace, and the tap was turned on full. She threw one of the Indian clubs at me but she was in a stew by that time, and it missed easily.

"I handed her over to Schmaltz, and she calmed down and told us all about it."

"Damn funny thing," Papa butted in. "Believe it or not, Barbara—"

"I'm telling this story," Dennis said firmly. "Now the thing began when the Rostrums went to Mrs. Markham and asked her who Barbara really was. She's a pretty good actress and she asked them what on earth they meant, with every sign of honest bewilderment. They explained that they had just finished reading a book which stated more or less positively that two blue-eyed parents could not produce a brown-eyed child. Mrs. Markham's eyes are a pale blue, of course, and the Rostrums knew that Mr. Markham's eyes had been blue as well.

"They had just seen Barbara in the dining room and noticed her dark eyes in the light of their new knowledge, and they declared they had almost fainted away.

"Mrs. Markham laughed at them and told them not to be silly enough to believe everything they read. But they were not satisfied and insisted that they were going to write to the author and tell him that they were prepared to prove to him that he was wrong.

"Mrs. Markham was in a spot. Barbara is not her daughter. She is Alvin's daughter, and Mrs. Markham took her when Barbara's mother died at the birth. Mrs. Markham had a daughter of her own, a few months older, and it was that child who died. But apparently there is money involved—a trust fund created by a cousin for the two daughters of Mrs. Markham and her sister—with a reversion to the survivor. Which meant that Mrs. Markham stood to lose both her daughter and the use and control of the money as well.

"The substitution of Barbara for her own child had been fairly easy. The doctor attending the sick child was a stranger, and Alvin and Mr. Markham were both away. Mrs. Markham simply gave the name of Alvin's child to be used on the death certificate and subsequently moved out of the neighborhood. Small babies change considerably in a month, and neither Mr. Markham nor Alvin ever suspected.

"Mrs. Markham returned to the old neighborhood after the death of her husband and opened up this place. She had felt absolutely safe through all these years, and the Rostrums, with their threat of exposure, never left her room alive. She struck them both down and placed them in front of the gas log. She locked her room and then turned the gas jet in the hall slightly on to account for the smell of gas if anyone commented.

"She went down to the drawing room for a while to plan her campaign and as soon as an opportunity presented itself she went through the kitchen and out to the yard, where she dug furiously in the tulip bed with

Alvin's shovel. She had intended to bury them and hoped they would simply be written off as lost, since no one would bother about them much anyway.

"But she was very nervous and when Miss Giddens dropped her shawl out of the window she decided to take it up and then see if the gas log had done its work. She forgot the shawl, in her excitement, and she discovered that there was a terrific smell of gas on the third floor. Luckily for her, there was no one about. Those on the fourth floor had gone up too early to notice it, and the rest were still downstairs or out. She rushed into her room, turned off the gas, and flung the windows wide, but the atmosphere forced her into the hall, where she probably wandered around, wringing her hands. After a while she remembered the shawl and the unfinished grave and went downstairs again. It was just at that time that you and Barbara were out in the yard, so she locked the back door in a panic and fled upstairs.

"The open windows had done away with a great deal of the gas, and she was able to go into her room and assure herself that the Rostrums were dead. But she had to wait. You were the only one to come up—she spoke to you in the hall—and the others did not come until five in the morning.

"She was nearly frantic by that time. She could not leave the bodies in the room and in the end she took them down to Miss Giddens, where she hoped they would not be discovered. She herself was the only person ever to go there. Even Evie was barred, since Mrs. Markham did the cleaning there herself.

"She commented on the Rostrums' disappearance the following day and that night she felt that she had a good opportunity to finish the business. Everyone went to bed but Barbara, you, and myself, and she figured that the three of us would be out until late. She finished digging the tulip bed and then showed panic again when she could not face bringing them down without wrapping them in something. She took down the portieres and planned to get them up again before anyone noticed.

"She wrapped the bodies while Miss Giddens chattered around her like a magpie, so that she did not hear us come in. She had Miss Imogene as far as the front hall before she heard us talking in the kitchen, and she dropped her burden in sheer terror. She collected herself sufficiently to drag the body into a dark corner of the drawing room and crouch beside it while we passed. But she was pretty well demoralized and she gave up the idea of the grave. The window was right beside her, and she pushed

Miss Imogene out onto the balcony, where she fell onto the iron seat. The portiere had fallen off, and Mrs. Markham simply folded it and threw it on top of the sideboard. She took a sleeping tablet, then, and went to bed.

"The next day she searched for the book but was unable to find it and later she searched for Miss Opal's diary, and that was when she tore the spare room apart. Miss Opal was in the habit of hiding things there, as Mrs. Markham knew, but she did not unearth the diary.

"Then she saw Alvin reading the book and she knew that she would have to get rid of him too.

"Miss Giddens turned out to be a disappointment to her at that time. As a rule, she could control the old lady and depend upon her to do and say as she was told. She had faithfully reported, per instructions, that a man had brought her two visitors, but Mrs. Markham had told her to expect another visitor but to say nothing, and instead, she had blabbed about it.

"However, Mrs. Markham took down the red drape and turned the gas jet in the hall half on, and then Alvin disappeared. She was worried, but not excessively so. She knew him pretty well and she felt sure that he would come back, as he did. Miss Giddens went for a walk at five in the morning, and he simply came back with her and was lucky enough not to be seen. He accompanied Miss Giddens to her room, possessed himself of the key to the door connecting Mary's room, and hid out first in one room and then the other, and sometimes in Miss Giddens' closet.

"Mrs. Markham must have known that he was back when you saw him in the drape and screamed. I suppose he was trying to get up to his room without being seen. She waited until he made another try and then threw the club at him—she was adept because she and her husband had played with Indian clubs as a hobby. The one she used was filled with lead and had been picked up as a curio.

"She dragged him into her room and much later that night she turned on the gas log and killed him. And then she burned Neville's hat. She got Alvin down to Miss Giddens' room, where she was appalled to find the door open and the light on. She just dropped him onto the chair and fled.

"She knew that Alvin had tried to give you a clue by leaving a picture of her husband in your room, but she did not suppose it would mean anything to you and she felt fairly safe. She had found the book in the drawing room and she had burned it, along with all the pictures of her husband. She heard you say that Barbara had worn the topaz brooch on the two occasions when her appearance had caused a mystifying consternation, so she threw that into the furnace, too, in case the stuff was discovered before it was destroyed. Apparently she had forgotten about the old picture in the cellar, and if Dodd had realized its importance he most probably could have cleared the thing up then and there.

"But Barbara was able to get another copy of the book from the library, and you read it, and her feeling of safety was shattered. She turned on the hall gas jet again and tried to enter your room, and as soon as you resisted she felt sure that you knew—and, of course, when Miss Giddens came out with the note there was no further doubt.

"So she had a shot at doing away with you, and I saved you. And I'll thank the old man not to forget it."

CHAPTER THIRTY-FIVE

DENNIS MADE A SIGN TO ME to get Papa out of the room, but Papa didn't see it and merely said comfortably, "I still don't understand why that red drape was in Diana's bureau."

"Alvin had eluded Mrs. Markham then," Dennis explained, trying to be patient, "and she had to hide the thing somewhere."

"He must have been a dumb goon," Papa said thoughtfully. "Alvin, I mean. Why didn't he go to the police instead of waiting around until she got him?"

"He was very fond of Barbara," Dennis said, "and he was desperately trying to avoid an open scandal."

I nodded. "He realized that Barbara had dark eyes that night when he dropped his cup and of course he knew that the Markhams had blue eyes. But he couldn't say anything about it to us."

"I believe he wanted to tell you, but he was balked."

"I balked him," I said with a faint sigh. "He was trying to get to his room disguised in that drape, and when I screamed he followed me in here. But I wouldn't shut up, so he hid under my bed. That's why the police never found him when they searched—they never thought of investigating the room I was screaming in. He lost the picture he had intended to show me, so he tore one out of Miss Giddens' album."

Papa frowned, still dissatisfied. "That wasn't the only search the police made though."

"It was easy enough, I think," Dennis said. "He dodged from Miss Giddens' room to Mary's, and back again."

"Why the hell didn't the damn police walk through the connecting door?" Papa boomed.

I laughed weakly and said, "I guess that was the same sort of search that they made for the red drape when it was under my arm."

"What's that?" said Papa.

"Quincy," Dennis broke in, with long suffering patience, "would you—"

"You can't address me like that," Papa shouted.

"All right, Bud," Dennis agreed. "I think it's a lousy name, myself. But will you kindly leave the room so that I can woo your daughter?"

"So that you can what?" Papa asked, shocked.

"Woo," I said. "What you did to Mother before you married her."

"I did no such thing," said Papa indignantly. "In fact, I hardly knew your mother before I married her. If he wants to do anything he can do it in front of my face and not behind my back."

"He wants to ask me to marry him," I explained.

Dennis said, "I'm not sure that I'd go as far as that—"

Papa raised his voice to a bellow that shook the very roof.

"You'll marry her and like it!" he roared.

THE END

About The Rue Morgue Press

The Rue Morgue vintage mystery line is designed to bring back into print those books that were favorites of readers between the turn of the century and the 1960s. The editors welcome suggests for reprints. To receive our catalog or make suggestions, write The Rue Morgue Press, P.O. Box 4119, Boulder, Colorado (1-800-669-6214). The Rue Morgue Press tries to keep all of its titles in print, though some books may go temporarily out of print for up to six months.

Catalog of Rue Morgue Press titles September 2002

Titles are listed by author. All books are quality trade paperbacks measuring 9 by 6 inches, usually with full-color covers and printed on paper designed not to yellow or deteriorate. These are permanent books.

Joanna Cannan. The books by this English writer are among our most popular titles. Modern reviewers favorably compared our two Cannan reprints with the best books of the Golden Age of detective fiction. "Worthy of being discussed in the same breath with an Agatha Christie or a Josephine Tey."—Sally Fellows, Mystery News. "First-rate Golden Age detection with a likeable detective, a complex and believable murderer, and a level of style and craft that bears comparison with Sayers, Allingham, and Marsh."—Jon L. Breen, *Ellery Queen's Mystery Magazine*. Set in the late 1930s in a village that was a fictionalized version of Oxfordshire, both titles feature young Scotland Yard inspector Guy Northeast. *They Rang Up the Police* (0-915230-27-5, 156 pages, $14.00) and *Death at The Dog* (0-915230-23-2, 156 pages, $14.00).

Glyn Carr. The author is really Showell Styles, one of the foremost English mountain-climbers of his era as well as one of that sport's most celebrated historians. Carr turned to crime fiction when he realized that mountains provided a ideal setting for committing murders. The 15 books featuring Shakespearean actor Abercrombie "Filthy" Lewker are set on peaks scattered around the globe, although the author returned again and again to his favorite climbs in Wales, where his first mystery, published in 1951, *Death on Milestone Buttress* (0-915230-29-1, 187 pages, $14.00), is set. Lewker is a marvelous Falstaffian character whose exploits have been praised by such discerning critics as Jacques Barzun and Wendell Hertig Taylor in *A Catalogue of Crime*.

Torrey Chanslor. *Our First Murder* (0-915230-50-X .$14.95) When a headless corpse is discovered in a Manhattan theatrical lodging house, who better to call in than the Beagle sisters? Sixty-five-year-old Amanda employs good old East Biddicutt common sense to run the agency, while her younger sister Lutie prowls the streets and nightclubs of 1940 Manhattan looking for clues. It's their first murder case since inheriting the Beagle Private Detective Agency from their older brother, but you'd never know the sisters had spent all of their lives knitting and tending to their garden in a small, sleepy upstate New York town. Lutie is a real charmer, who learned her craft by reading scores of lurid detective novels borrowed from the East Biddicut Circulating Library. With her younger cousin Marthy in tow, Lutie is totally at ease as she questions suspects and orders vintage champagne. Of course, if trouble pops up, there's always that pearl-handled revolver tucked away in her purse.

Our First Murder is a charming hybrid of the private eye, traditional, and cozy mystery, written in 1940 by a woman who earned two Caldecott nominations for her illustrations of children's books.

Clyde B. Clason. Clason has been praised not only for his elaborate plots and skillful use of the locked room gambit but also for his scholarship. He may be one of the few mystery authors—and no doubt the first—to provide a full bibliography of his sources. *The Man from Tibet* (0-915230-17-8, 220 pages, $14.00) is one of his best (selected in 2001 in *The History of Mystery* as one of the 25 great amateur detective novels of all time) and highly recommended by the dean of locked room mystery scholars, Robert Adey, as "highly original." It's also one of the first popular novels to make use of Tibetan culture.

Joan Coggin. *Who Killed the Curate?* Meet Lady Lupin Lorrimer Hastings, the young, lovely, scatterbrained and kindhearted newlywed wife to the vicar of St. Marks Parish in Glanville, Sussex. When it comes to matters clerical, she literally doesn't know Jews from Jesuits and she's hopelessly at sea at the meetings of the Mothers' Union, Girl Guides, or Temperance Society but she's determined to make husband Andrew proud of her—or, at least, not to embarass him too badly. So when Andrew's curate is poisoned, Lady Lupin enlists the help of her old society pals, Duds and Tommy Lethbridge, as well as Andrew's nephew, a British secret service agent, to get at the truth. Lupin refuses to believe Diane Lloyd, the 38-year-old author of children's and detective stories could have done the deed, and casts her net out over the other parishioners. All the suspects seem so nice, much more so than the victim, and Lupin announces she'll help the killer escape if only he or she confesses. Set at Christmas 1937 and first published in England in 1944, this is the first American appearance of *Who Killed the Curate?* "Marvelous."—*Deadly Pleasures* (0-915230-44-5, $14.00).

Manning Coles. The two English writers who collaborated as Coles are best known for those witty spy novels featuring Tommy Hambledon, but they also wrote four delightful—and funny—ghost novels. *The Far Traveller* (0-915230-35-6, 154 pages, $14.00) is a stand-alone novel in which a film company unknowingly hires the ghost of a long-dead German graf to play himself in a movie. "I laughed until I hurt. I liked it so much, I went back to page 1 and read it a second time."—Peggy Itzen, *Cozies, Capers & Crimes*. The other three books feature two cousins, one English, one American, and their spectral pet monkey who got a little drunk and tried to stop—futilely and fatally—a German advance outside a small French village during the 1870 Franco-Prussian War. Flash forward to the 1950s where this comic trio of friendly ghosts rematerialize to aid relatives in danger in *Brief Candles* (0-915230-24-0, 156 pages, $14.00), *Happy Returns* (0-915230-31-3, 156 pages, $14.00) and *Come and Go* (0-915230-34-8, 155 pages, $14.00).

Norbert Davis. There have been a lot of dogs in mystery fiction, from Baynard Kendrick's guide dog to Virginia Lanier's bloodhounds, but there's never been one quite like Carstairs. Doan, a short, chubby Los Angeles private eye, won Carstairs in a crap game, but there never is any question as to who the boss is in this relationship. Carstairs isn't just any Great Dane. He is so big that Doan figures he really ought to be considered another species. He scorns baby talk and belly rubs—unless administered by a pretty girl—and growls whenever Doan has a drink. His full name is Dougal's Laird Carstairs and as a sleuth he rarely barks up the wrong tree. He's down in Mexico with Doan, ostensibly to convince a missing fugitive that he would do well to stay put, in *The Mouse in the Mountain* (0-915230-41-0, 151 pages, $14.00), first published in 1943 and followed by two other Doan and Carstairs novels. *Staff pick* at The Sleuth of Baker Street in Toronto, Murder by the Book in Houston and The Poisoned Pen in Scotsdale. Four star review in *Romantic Times*. "A laugh a minute romp…hilarious dialogue and descriptions…utterly engaging, downright fun read…fetch this one! Highly recommended."—Michele A. Reed, *I Love a Mystery.* "Deft, charming…unique…one of my top ten all time favorite novels."—Ed Gorman, *Mystery Scene*. The second book, *Sally's in the Alley* (0-915230-46-1, $14.00), was equally well-received. *Publishers Weekly*: "Norbert Davis committed suicide in 1949, but his incomparable crime-fighting duo, Doan, the tippling private eye, and Carstairs, the huge and preternaturally clever Great Dane, march on in a re-release of the 1943 *Sally's in the Alley*. Doan's on a government-sponsored mission to find an ore deposit in the Mojave Desert…in an old-fashioned romp that matches its bloody crimes with belly laughs." The editor of *Mystery Scene* chimed in: "I love Craig Rice. Davis is her equal." "The funniest P.I. novel ever written."—*The Drood Review*.

Elizabeth Dean. Dean wrote only three mysteries, but in Emma Marsh she created one of the first independent female sleuths in the genre. Written in the screwball style of the 1930s, *Murder is a Collector's Item* (0-915230-19-4, $14.00) is described in a review in *Deadly Pleasures* by award-winning mystery writer Sujata Massey as a story that "froths over with the same effervescent humor as the best Hepburn-Grant films." Like the second book in the trilogy, *Murder is a Serious Business* (0-915230-28-3, 254 pages, $14.95), it's set in a Boston antique store just as the Great Depression is drawing to a close. *Murder a Mile High* (0-915230-39-9, 188 pages, $14.00), moves to the Central City Opera House in the Colorado mountains, where Emma has been summoned by am old chum, the opera's reigning diva. Emma not only has to find a murderer, she may also have to catch a Nazi spy. "Fascinating."—*Romantic Times.*

Constance & Gwenyth Little. These two Australian-born sisters from New Jersey have developed almost a cult following among mystery readers. Critic Diane Plumley, writing in *Dastardly Deeds*, called their 21 mysteries "celluloid comedy written on paper." Each book, published between 1938 and 1953, was a stand-alone, but there was no mistaking a Little heroine. She hated housework, wasn't averse to a little gold-digging (so long as she called the shots), and couldn't help antagonizing cops and potential beaux. The Rue Morgue Press intends to reprint all of their books. Currently available: *The Black Thumb* (O-915230-48-8, 155 pages, $14.00), *The Black Coat* (0-915230-40-2, 155 pages, $14.00), *Black Corridors* (0-915230-33-X, 155 pages, $14.00), *The Black Gloves* (0-915230-20-8, 185 pages, $14.00), *Black-Headed Pins* (0-915230-25-9, 155 pages, $14.00), *The Black Honeymoon* (0-915230-21-6, 187 pages, $14.00), *The Black Paw* (0-915230-37-2, 156 pages, $14.00), *The Black Stocking* (0-915230-30-5, 154 pages, $14.00), *Great Black Kanba* (0-915230-22-4, 156 pages, $14.00), and *The Grey Mist Murders* (0-915230-26-7, 153 pages, $14.00), and *The Black Eye* (0-915230-45-3, 154 pages, $14.00). Look for *The Black Shrouds* (0-915230-52-6, 155 pages, $14.00) in autumn 2002.

Marlys Millhiser. Our only non-vintage mystery, *The Mirror* (0-915230-15-1, 303 pages, $17.95) is our all-time bestselling book, now in a sixth printing. How could you not be intrigued by a novel in which "you find the main character marrying her own grandfather and giving birth to her own mother," as one reviewer put it of this supernatural, time-travel (sort-of) piece of wonderful make-believe set both in the mountains above Boulder, Colorado, at the turn of the century and in the city itself in 1978. Internet book services list scores of rave reviews from readers who often call it the "best book I've ever read."

James Norman. The marvelously titled *Murder, Chop Chop* (0-915230-16-X, 189 pages, $13.00) is a wonderful example of the eccentric detective novel. "The book has the butter-wouldn't-melt-in-his-mouth cool of Rick in *Casablanca.*"—*The Rocky Mountain News.* "Amuses the reader no end."—*Mystery News.* "This long out-of-print masterpiece is intricately plotted, full of eccentric characters and very humorous indeed. Highly recommended."—*Mysteries by Mail.* Meet Gimiendo Hernandez Quinto, a gigantic Mexican who once rode with Pancho Villa and who now trains *guerrilleros* for the Nationalist Chinese government when he isn't solving murders. At his side is a beautiful Eurasian known as Mountain of Virtue, a woman as dangerous to men as she is irresistible. First published in 1942.

Sheila Pim. *Ellery Queen's Mystery Magazine* said of these wonderful Irish village mysteries that Pim "depicts with style and humor everyday life." *Booklist* said they were in "the best tradition of Agatha Christie." *Common or Garden Crime* (0-915230-36-4, 157 pages, $14.00) is set in neutral Ireland during World War II when Lucy Bex must use her knowledge of gardening to keep the wrong person from going to the gallows. Beekeeper Edward Gildea uses his knowledge of bees and plants to do the same thing in *A Hive of Suspects* (0-915230-38-0, 155 pages, $14.00). *Creeping Venom* (0-915230-42-9, 155 pages, $14.00) mixes politics and religion into a deadly mixture. *A Brush with Death* (0-915230-49-6) grafts a clever art scam onto the stem of a gardening mystery.

Craig Rice. *Home Sweet Homicide.* This marvelous funny and utterly charming tale (set in 1942 and first published in 1944) of three children who "help" their widowed mystery writer mother solve a real-life murder and nab a handsome cop boyfriend along the way made just about every list of the best mysteries for the first half of the 20th century, including: The Haycraft-Queen Cornerstone list, probably the most prestigious honor role in the history of crime fiction, James Sandoe's Reader's Guide to Crime, and Mevlyn Barnes' *Murder in Print.* Rice was of course best known for her screwball mystery comedies featuring Chicago criminal attorney John J. Malone. *Home Sweet Homicide* is a delightful cozy mystery partially based on Rice's own home life. It was filmed in 1946 with Peggy Ann Garner (who earned a special Oscar that year for her work as a juvenile lead), Randolph Scott, and Dean Stockwell, whose performance as Archie, the young son of mystery writer Marian Carstairs, captivated the hearts of the movie-going public. Negotiations are underway for a possible remake of this classic movie. Rice, the first mystery writer to appear on the cover of *Time*, died in 1957 at the age of 49. For more information on the author see the introduction to *Home Sweet Homicide*. Rice and her real-life office provided the inspiration for the cover to this new edition of *Home Sweet Homicide*. 0-915230-53-4, $14.95

Charlotte Murray Russell. Spinster sleuth Jane Amanda Edwards tangles with a murderer and Nazi spies in *The Message of the Mute Dog* (0-915230-43-7, 156 pages, $14.00), a culinary cozy set just before Pearl Harbor. "Perhaps the mother of today's cozy."—*The Mystery Reader*. Our earlier title, *Cook Up a Crime*, is currently out of print.

Juanita Sheridan. Sheridan was one of the most colorful figures in the history of detective fiction, as you can see from Tom and Enid Schantz's introduction to *The Chinese Chop* (0-915230-32-1, 155 pages, $14.00). Her books are equally colorful, as well as showing how mysteries with female protagonists began changing after World War II. The postwar housing crunch finds Janice Cameron, newly arrived in New York City from Hawaii, without a place to live until she answers an ad for a roommate. It turns out the advertiser is an acquaintance from Hawaii, Lily Wu, whom critic Anthony Boucher (for whom Bouchercon, the World Mystery Convention, is named) described as an "exquisitely blended product of Eastern and Western cultures" and the only female sleuth that he "was devotedly in love with," citing "that odd mixture of respect for her professional skills and delight in her personal charms." First published in 1949, this ground-breaking book was the first of four to feature Lily and be told by her Watson, Janice, a first-time novelist. "Highly recommended."—*I Love a Mystery*. "This well-written. . .enjoyable variant of the boarding house whodunit and a vivid portrait of the post WWII New York City housing shortage, puts to lie the common misconception that strong, self-reliant, non-spinster-or-comic sleuths didn't appear on the scene until the 1970s. Chinese-American Lily Wu and her novelist Watson, Janice Cameron, are young and feminine but not dependent on men."—*Ellery Queen's Mystery Magazine*. The first book in the series to be set in Hawaii is *The Kahuna Killer* (0-915230-47-X, 154 pages, $14.00). "Janice Cameron's return to Hawaii is 'the signal to set off a chain of events which [bring] discord and catastrophe,' as well as murder. Originally published five decades ago (thought it doesn't feel like it), this detective story featuring charming Chinese sleuth Lily Wu has the friends and foster sisters investigating mysterious events—blood on an ancient altar, pagan rights, and the appearance of a kahuna (a witch doctor)—and the death of a sultry hula girl in 1950s Oahu."—*Publishers Weekly*. Third in the series is *The Mamo Murders* (0915230-51-8, $14.00), set on a Maui cattle ranch.